I0677923

THE CHAOS WITHIN

Ashima Chalia has a degree in law from the prestigious National Law University, Jodhpur. Having successfully worked for over three years in corporate consultancy with one of the leading consultancy firms, where she dealt with multinational and Fortune 500 clients, Ashima realized that her true passion lies in creative writing. In order to pursue her passion she gave up her flourishing corporate career and dedicated her time to writing her first work of fiction, *The Chaos Within*. She also has a keen interest in fashion journalism and holds a certificate in fashion journalism from London College of Fashion. In addition to penning her first book, Ashima writes extensively on current fashion trends in her blog 'Ashima Wandering'. You can know more about Ashima by visiting her website: www.ashimachalia.com.

THE
CHAOS
WITHIN

Ashima Chalia

RUPA

Published by
Rupa Publications India Pvt. Ltd 2015
7/16, Ansari Road, Daryaganj
New Delhi 110002

Sales Centres:

Allahabad Bengaluru Chennai
Hyderabad Jaipur Kathmandu
Kolkata Mumbai

This is a work of fiction. Names, characters, places and incidents are
either the product of the author's imagination or are used fictitiously and
any resemblance to any actual person, living or dead,
events or locales is entirely coincidental.

ISBN: 978-81-291-34783

First impression 2015

10 9 8 7 6 5 4 3 2 1

The moral right of the author has been asserted.

Printed at Repro Knowledgecast Limited, Thane

To my 'Significant Other'
who made this book possible with the bribe of
chocolates and with the threat of a ban on them

Contents

Prologue

'Yet another reunion! Is it not enough that I do this every year, now they bhont something bhich is a little different,' thought Mr Banerjee, silently swearing to himself. As head of administration at St. Magnum's College, he was in charge of everything from admissions down to even why a toilet wasn't flushing properly. The job, which he had held for more than sixteen years, had ruined the entire joy and nostalgia of reunions for him. For Mr Banerjee, reunions were routine events that took place every year—just that each time it was different group of 30-something youngsters hovering around. As if this was not enough, the 'new age' Vice Chancellor Mr Shantanu Pandit had asked his dedicated head of administration to make this reunion a 'little different'.

'Rascal! Wants to bring a change in the college, wants to make it—how did he put it—more bhibrant. Orrey, it's a college not a phub, although these days who can tell the difference? Kali Mata, bhat bhill happen to this generation,' cribbed Mr Banerjee, who couldn't control his Bengali accent even in his thoughts. *'Another year, another reunion,'* he muttered to himself, picked up the paper and scrunched up his eyebrows ignoring his glasses lying in front of him, in his constant effort to believe his youth, *'Let's*

see bhich bhone is it this time—class of 2003!'

He took a long look at the list of graduates and yawned. Suddenly, as if jolted, he looked over the list again, grabbed his glasses, thrusted them on his face and then checked the list twice in disbelief. *'Kali Mata tum kothi gele! This batch is the Fiasco Five batch, how will I survive them again! Weren't three years of pain and torture enough? I will have to renew my ulcer medicines by the end of this reunion.*

Finally, after looking at the list for an hour in disbelief and cursing his gods, Mr Banerjee's highly active grey cells (courtesy his love of fish, which he nearly included in his every meal) came up with a brilliant idea to make the reunion look a 'little different' with minimal work from his part. He took out a five-year-old reunion template from the college records that read:

Dear _____

With great love and affection, St. Magnum College invites you and your family to the reunion of the batch of 1998. Please bring along your appetite for a gala function sprinkled with your fondest memories.

Vice Chancellor

Mr Banerjee undertook the tedious task of changing the year on the invite and adding another line about the ceremonial affair that this reunion was going to be. Voila! His invitation for the reunion was ready. Proud of himself, he got up to take it to the VC, but changed his mind and decided to sit on it for a few more days. After all, even a genius like him would need at least a couple of days to come up with an invitation this elegant. With a sly smile on his face, Mr Banerjee turned off the computer, sipped his black tea without sugar and relaxed on his wooden chair. While doing so, he looked at the rickety fan and thought about the day when the Fiasco Five nearly killed him with one of their harmless little jokes.

≈

A Month Later

Damodar looked around the room one last time. He made sure his suicide note would be impossible to miss by anyone entering the room. As he brought the gun to his temple his hands shook, and he wondered how long his body would be left in this dingy little room. He knew it wouldn't be long since his landlord would soon visit to demand the last six months' rent and the money that Damodar had borrowed from him. *'Little did the poor landlord know that not only was he not going to get his money back, but was about to drown in a world's worth of trouble. After all, it was with his money that I bought this unregistered, unlicensed gun,'* Damodar thought to himself.

Gathering his courage, he almost pressed the trigger, but instead of a gunshot, he heard a doorbell. Realizing that he was still alive, he pondered whether he should open the door or not. *'For all you know, the landlord may have come earlier than expected,'* thought Damodar and tightened his grip on the gun once again. But as if Kali Mata was a taking personal interest in the ulcers Mr Banerjee was about to get, the guy at the door shouted 'Postman!' Damodar's thoughts instantly swirled and he forgot all about the gun and his plans of freeing himself from his sad life. He mentally scanned the list of the handful of people he knew and couldn't think of anyone who liked him enough to send him a letter. He got up to open the door, but on second thought, put the gun on the bedside table, out of sight. Unable to control his curiosity any longer, he opened the door and took the elegant crimson envelope from the frustrated postman. The envelope was embossed in gold, and bore the unmistakable logo of St. Magnum College. He tore open the envelope and read hurriedly with rapt attention, since he wanted to return to his ever-so-important task.

However, by the end of it there was only one thought that lingered in his empty mind: his death could wait a little...

1

The Road Less Travelled

KRISH PARKED HIS limited edition Mercedes Benz SLR McLaren with a skid and rushed towards the ballroom. He wasn't particularly late, but he figured that now that he was here, he might as well roam around and look at his alma mater. Walking up to the ballroom, he saw that the college had gone out of its way to make this day special, with grand lighting, and in turn had made them sport formal wear. Smirking to himself, he decided to take the same shortcut he used to as a student and take a trip down memory lane. Back then, he had considered every good-looking girl in the college a conquest, and he had never lost a battle. Nothing had changed for him in a decade, his lifestyle remained the same: endless one-night stands, a string of meaningless relationships, and no responsibilities apart from the family business which, of course, belonged to him after his father's death. He knew that there were many who frowned upon his lifestyle, but oh, how he loved it! A life of complete freedom; no one to question his choices, no one to second-guess his every step.

On the path to the ballroom, he strolled past the old shed, *'Why would they keep this thing still standing, it is positively falling apart... And apart from storing a lot of sentimental junk it wasn't used for anything or by anyone else, other than maybe the couples who were looking to get away from the world.'* He smiled slyly. *'Was it that bad even when we were here?'* he thought to himself. *'Well, maybe I just didn't care because of the perks it offered. Boy! How many great moments I have had here.'* He smirked at the thought of all the girls with whom he had shared intimate moments in the shed, and how all of them had thought that they were his one true love. And how with some, even he had believed that they were indeed his true love, or soul mate, or whatever romantic crap the movies try to sell. But no matter how much each one of them wanted to pin him down, he always wiggled out.

Even as a child he had always possessed a special charm over women. He had always been soft-spoken, well-mannered and well-behaved. He had to be—his father had paid plenty of money for him to be sent to the best of schools, and he had been taught how to be the best at everything. Heck, by the age of ten not only could he eat with all the silverware, but could even lay down a table which would have given any five-star restaurant a run for its money. Krish smiled at the memories and decided to move on towards his destination, estimating that everyone must have arrived by now. Since the time he had received the invitation, he had only thought about the faces he was dying to see, but now that he was finally here, he remembered all the other faces that, well, may not be very happy to see him. *'Well! Que sera sera, if they still hang on to the past it's their problem not mine, and let's face it, apart from a few awkward glances and conversations, my evening will be spent mostly with the Fiasco Five.'*

Lost in his own thoughts he reached the steps of the ballroom and started to look for a friendly face. Insead, he found only the ordinary 'janta' and some of his lovely 'shed-mates', as his friends called them, most of whom seemed to have failed to carry on their charming looks post marriage. Ordinarily, he was not the kind of person who was prone to anxiety, however, since the time he had stepped on the campus, there had been a sense of foreboding in his heart. He sighed and reassured himself—that the feeling was probably just because it had been a long while since he had seen his best friends—and he proceeded inside.

The ballroom was decorated quite differently than what he remembered. When they had been in charge, it had had a fun and casual theme and not this stuffy formal one, he thought, loosening his tie a little. Although Krish knew he had been born with super good looks, awesome height—almost touching 6 ft 2—complementing dark brown hair, athletic physique, courtesy his parents and their exclusive gym and club memberships (he also knew that he could be wearing leaves for crying out loud and still look, well not to be immodest, drop dead gorgeous), there was just something about ties that always made him uncomfortable, almost tangled up. It always reminded him of his father getting ready for one of his business meetings which of course were always more important for him resulting in the numerous times he had left him to the care of one of his nannies.

Returning to reality, he looked around the ballroom which was a mix of sophistication and class. Finally, after critiquing the entire enterprise and examining all the faces that were present, he decided not to brace the curious glances which were already picking him apart as if he was a lab rat. Silently and politely smiling at some people around he took a seat at the end of the room, not too far from the bar, which gave him a vantage point from which he could eye every girl that entered the ballroom. Taking deep breaths, he calmed himself down, took out the bolts from his pocket and started to play with them.

'Can I get you anything, Sir?' a waitress asked Krish with a polite smile plastered on her face. Looking at her from head to toe, he gave her a charming smile and said, 'Single malt with a single cube of ice. And sweetheart, keep it coming, I promise you won't regret it.' He trailed her with his eyes as she walked to the bar and back with a glass. As she did, she glanced at the dirty bolts resting on the crisp and white linen cloth and cringed at the thought of the rust marks they would leave behind. Almost reading her mind, Krish smiled to himself and thought about the countless number of crisp business shirts he had destroyed due to his habit of carrying these bolts everywhere.

No sooner had he taken a sip of the perfect single malt, he saw Samrat Dholakia aka Dholki walk in. They exchanged a glance, and by his look, Dholki made it clear beyond doubt, as expected, that he too disapproved of the theme. Perhaps by now he just disapproves of anything and everything that takes him away from his business. Krish couldn't tell.

And just like that, Krish started to think about the first day he had met Dholki, in fact, the day he had met all his best friends.

≈

2

The Fiasco Five

As they moved towards Mr Banerjee's office, Krish immediately usurped command and started to dictate as he pointed towards Dholki and Kabir, 'Listen, we three will go inside and get started, you two stand out here and don't let anyone come inside.'

'And how do you suggest we do that, gorgeous?' Kamakshii asked, annoyed.

'Well! You know…use your charms,' Krish said with a sly smile, while making suggestive gestures with his eyebrows, but stopped once he saw Kamakshii's expression. 'Okay, so let's go before someone actually comes,' Krish wrapped up quickly.

Leaving Mahi and Kamakshii outside the room, the three of them went in and started looking for something to take back as a trophy. Once inside, Samrat started to ramble on about how it was a bad idea to stand up against the seniors, how he was going to be expelled, how his whole life was doomed and that he should have never agreed to this.

Turning a deaf ear to his ranting, Kabir asked 'Oye! What

do you reckon we should take? The computer keyboard?'

'What? The keyboard? No way... They'll kill us, definitely. No, I can't do that. We need to leave—we need to leave right now. Let's just go and nobody will know,' Samrat prattled on hysterically.

Krish, rolling his eyes, walked to Samrat, grabbed him by his shoulders and said, 'Listen Dholakia! We can't go out. They will continue to torment us all through our college years, it will be hell. We will be the laughing stock of the college. Do you want to go through all that or do you want to lay it to rest once and for all...?' Samrat didn't answer. 'Okay then. So, we will do this and do it fast.' Listening to Krish, Samrat finally calmed down, and nodded vigorously.

'Let's concentrate and think—we definitely can't take the keyboard. We need something symbolic of this college, something that will make them shut up once and for all,' Krish said, trying to find something that would suffice.

As if on cue, Mahi peeped in and inquired, 'Are you guys done yet?'

Before Krish could respond, Kabir chipped in, 'No, we need a little more time. Are you guys okay? Is anybody coming?'

Clearly irritated, Mahi said, 'Would you guys mind hurrying up? The bell is going to ring anytime and I don't think anything I can do will distract them.'

'Oh, don't underestimate your potential, darling,' Krish smirked. And then he added, 'Lighten up sweetheart, it's just a joke. Anyway, it's so hot in here we don't need you to elevate the temperature. I would've switched on the fan if I wasn't so afraid it might just fall on our heads.'

'Wait, the fan, we can take the fan!' Krish said looking up, trying to estimate how much time it would take to bring it down. He dragged a chair under the fan and started to climb on it. 'Will you guys give me a hand?' he asked, looking at Kabir and Samrat, who, if not for the look of utter disbelief on their faces, would have passed for statues.

Kabir, the first to recover, started to shout, 'You've completely lost your mind! It's one thing to get something symbolic, but it's completely different to steal college property. And yeah, I do want to walk with my head up straight, but I would like it better if it was still attached to my body, which it wouldn't be, if anybody finds out!'

Samrat, who had pinned himself against the wall like a lizard, croaked with fear, 'He is absolutely right, being ragged and still being in this college is better than not being in this college at all. If we leave right now, nobody will know. I am not a part of this anymore. I am leaving right now. Just move. You are the reason we all got into this mess.' 'I can't believe you guys! We all decided that this was the right thing to do. In fact, it was the only thing to do. Nobody is leaving—we are all in this together. Now, do any of you have any other ideas? If not, then we are going to stick with the Pretty Boy's plan,' Kamakshii said barging in. 'Okay, so I am staying in here, and that means that we need someone outside. Now, as Samrat looks as if he might just pee himself right here he can't go outside, so Kabir you go outside and be nonchalant. And please wipe that love-sick puppy look off your face,' Kamakshii said.

All five of them looked at each other and then moved. Krish looked at Kamakshii as he had never looked at any other girl before, impressed by her ability to hold her nerve. He took a Swiss knife out of his pocket and then started to unscrew the fan, bolt by bolt, which was all the more difficult because they were rusted to the core. By the time he reached the last bolt, more than fifteen minutes had passed and they were running out of time.

As he struggled with the last bolt, and Kamakshii and Samrat held their breaths while steadying the chair, Kabir barged in, 'Heads up, Banerjee is coming. We need to get out now.'

'What! But all we have is the bolts! We need the fan! But this last bolt is really rusted and I can't get it to budge,' Krish exclaimed, hurrying up.

'We need to go right now. If we don't get out right now, leave alone the seniors, even the teachers will rag us for our whole term,' Kabir exclaimed, panicking.

'No, we need to get this, I need to get this... I am not leaving without it. You guys go, just go, I can handle it,' Krish yelled, struggling with the bolt frantically.

'Listen Pretty Boy, we have done our best. There's no point in fighting this, we need to go right now, and if we don't, we will all be expelled,' Kamakshii yelled as she took Krish's hand and yanked him roughly making him almost fall face-first. At lightning speed, Kabir grabbed the chair and put it back into its place.

They ran as fast as their feet could carry them before Mr Banarjee popped into the room. They ran till they reached the field behind the classroom, and flopped on all fours gasping for air. Krish clutched his chest and tried to speak, but all that came out were wheezing sounds.

Once they had collected themselves, they decided to go to the mess and act as normally as they could. As they stepped in, it seemed as though every head turned to follow them.

Walking slowly, they reached the dining room and sat down at the nearest table. 'Does anybody else get the feeling that we are being talked about? Do they know about what we were trying to do? Do you think the seniors told the teachers?' Samrat started babbling again.

'No Dholakia, it's not possible. They can't tell anyone or they will also get in trouble. They have no proof. There's a higher chance of you screwing this up than them. For now, till this is over, you will stay with me and be happy about it,' Krish said.

'Will all of you just relax? I am sure we're just over-reacting, that's it. Everybody is staring at us because we were brave enough to stand up to the seniors. Let's just get on with our day, nobody knows what we did. Let's talk about something else,' Kamakshii snapped.

'Yeah, let's talk about the fresher's party tomorrow night. What are you planning to wear?' Mahi asked, trying to change the subject.

'Aiyo, god please kill me now,' Kamakshii breathed, just loud enough to reach Krish's ear, who smiled and winked at her. 'Sweetheart, I don't really care. I guess I will just throw something on. Besides, I don't have time for anything else, the basketball try-outs are tomorrow.'

'Heads up guys! Vikrant is coming,' Kabir hushed them and pointed at a burly-looking guy who looked as if he had been yanked out of a Rocky Balboa movie. He wore a t-shirt so tight that it could have passed off as second skin if not for the colour orange.

'So studs, what do you have to show for yourselves? Or do you guys concede defeat?' Vikrant asked, thumping hard on Samrat's back, in an accent as thick as Rocky's.

Glancing around at the table, Krish saw that Samrat had already started shaking with fear. He knew that he had to act fast or else they would never be able to survive. He yanked out the bolts and put them on the table for everyone to see.

'What's this champ? Screws from your brain?' Vikrant teased and then smirked at his own intelligence.

'Actually, they are from Mr Banerjee's office fan. You wanted something symbolic, and here it is. Anybody could get a pen or a notebook or even his coat, but this is a part of the college. Go ahead, you can touch them if you want. So I guess it's over now, huh?' said Krish casually.

Vikrant picked up the screws and gave them a hard look, trying to decide what to make of it. His face twisted in anger as he spoke through his teeth, 'Do you guys think we are mad, or do you think we were born yesterday? These screws could be from anywhere. For all I know, you could have bought them from a junkyard.'

As if God himself was taking their side, Vikrant's friends walked in laughing hysterically. He waved them over to the table and was just about to show them the screws, when one of them spoke, 'Oh, you should've seen his face. Serves him right, he never lets us have any fun.'

'Whom are you guys talking about?' Vikrant asked.

'Banerjee. Haven't you heard? His office fan collapsed as soon as he switched it on. You should've seen it! The fan was swaying from a wire all over the room and Banerjee was shrieking in a corner asking Kali Mata to save him. Dumb fellow! The fan was moving so slowly, even if he had marched around it, he would have been safe, but he kept yelling for help.'

'Anyway, why did you call us here?' asked his classmate.

As Vikrant explained what had happened, the five of them shifted uncomfortably underneath their gazes. They knew that this would be the end of it, the seniors would report them and then they would be sent home. But lo and behold, the seniors turned towards them and smiled. Vikrant gave the bolts back to Krish and said, 'Your secret's safe with us, not to worry. We aren't snitches and you guys have my word. Nobody is going to rag you anymore.' And with that they formed a new bond which lasted them for years to come but not the one as strong as the one which formed between the five of them. Nobody knows how the whole college came to know about their deed, but by the end of the day, they had earned the name Fiasco Five.

3

Mr Pauper Prince

'HEY MAN! LONG time, how are you?' Samrat greeted Krish from almost two tables away. As soon as he reached the table, Krish got up and gave him a crushing hug. 'Wow! Man, I know, it's almost been six years. I think the last time we met was in that Asian Entrepreneur Conference in Japan.'

After the usual pleasantries were out of the way, both of them sat down smiling at each other. 'So what's new in life? Any marriage plans...?' Samrat probed partially out of politeness and partially because he just wanted to tease him as he already knew the answer even before he had asked—he knew his friend even after so many years had passed. Samrat had heard others say that the best years of anyone's life are those that one spends in college, and that the friends that you make in those years will be the closest to your heart He had always thought that was a load of crap. However, with the recent turn of events in his life, he was forced to revisit his beliefs.

'Dude, this looks like an Armani, now I am officially jealous of you,' Krish chimed, not able to hide his admiration for Dholki's suit. Dholki smiled and sighed knowing fully well that if Krish wanted he could buy ten of the same suits and then just for the kick of it make his so called team of advisors wear them as uniform. 'Look at you, dude. I am so proud of you, Dholakia. You have really done well for yourself, exactly what you set out to do. You have changed, man...I can't believe this is the same guy who fought with the pizza delivery guy for the change he owed you. It was hilarious, I mean I had almost expected you to say to him *"Ik rupiye ki kimat tum kya jaano,* pizza babu."'

Dholki retorted laughing, 'Yeah, well, it is quite a contrast from the last time we were all here. All through my childhood and college days all I could afford was what I used to buy once a year on my birthday, and that too from a local garment shop where dad knew the owner well enough to get a heavy discount. And now that I can afford it, why not indulge in some sinful spending?' added Samrat with pride, recollecting the tough times his parents had gone through to get him into an institute like St. Magnum's. He shuddered at the thought of his father having to mortgage their meagre two-bedroom house to take the education loan, and even his mother had to work over-time trying to pay it off. Not able to stop the memories from rushing in, Samrat's mind flashed to more recent images of how he had fulfilled his father's dream by sending his parents on a world tour, and how they now had a four-bedroom apartment in one of the most posh localities of Ahmedabad. He was jolted back to reality by a tap on his shoulder. 'Hey man, are you even here?' Krish said. 'Please don't start thinking about your work... I know you are a hotshot in your company, but I am sure that they can survive without you for at least a dinner, yaar. Seriously, sometimes I wonder how Karuna managed to be married to you for so many years. How long has it been since you got married?' Krish groaned.

'Seven years this August,' Samrat answered, even though his thoughts had started to wander off again. He pulled himself back to reality and decided to enjoy the evening. As if trying to prove a point, his eyes scanned the faces which at a point of time in his life were more familiar to him than even his own.

'Abbey Dholki, look it's Tanmay!' Krish said. 'Oh c'mon! Don't tell me you don't remember him. Tanmay...Tanmay Sharma!' Krish emphasized the name as if Samrat had forgotten his own. 'Abbey! How can you forget him? He used to pee in people's rooms when he got drunk. Don't you remember how hilarious it was when he peed in Kabir's room?'

'Of course!' Samrat exclaimed, remembering the infamous night when they had played a prank on their friend Kabir. And as if a lightning bolt had hit him, he asked, 'He doesn't know that we were the ones who...? That we had....?'

'What? That we were the ones who led him to Kabir's room? You have met Kabir right? The 6-foot 2-inch tall freak who used to bench-press double his body weight and run five kilometres everyday while we were busy sleeping. No, I love my life, and besides, who was gonna tell him? I mean the only other guy involved was so flushed he didn't even remember how to pee correctly,' Krish snickered.

They both laughed at the sheer insanity of it. Samrat, who had just welled up thinking about the hilarity of the situation, wondered how long it had been since he had felt this elated.

Samrat remembered how Krish would get his five-figure monthly allowance, while the others would be happy to get a thousand rupees extra in some months. They would all chip in to buy alcohol (although Krish and Kabir used to put in a bit more without telling him, Samrat always knew and promised himself that someday he would make it up to them). They would sneak in the bottles early in the morning, from Krish's car to Krish's room, not because they would get caught by the warden, which was a criterion too, but rather to shield it from all the booze-deprived boys. Samrat thought how by "they", it usually just meant Kabir, since he was the only one stupid enough to get up at five in morning to workout. As long as he was being stupid, why should they give up their million-dollar sleep?

As he was reminiscing about college, he couldn't help but remember the night when that infamous incident had happened. Not only did they play a prank on Kabir, but they got to uncover secrets too, secrets which had made them realize that even after spending so much time together, they knew so little about each other. He knew after that day the meaning of the modern day mantra, '*Har ik friend kamina hota hai*'. He remembered how Krish had blown almost twenty-five grand that night on booze, which wasn't a big deal for him, of course, considering his pocket money, but this time he had done it only for the three of them. For Samrat, that night meant a lot.

≈

4

The Drinking Night

SAMRAT HAD BEEN lying on his cot and admiring the downpour from the little window in his room. On days like these he liked to hole up in his room, with a plate of Joshiji's special occasion pakoras and a cup of tea. While in other colleges students cribbed about their mess food, Samrat considered himself to be among the few lucky ones to have a college whose mess food was above average (i.e., they could not only see the dal in dal fry, but it also tasted like it too). But then again, he was a boy who had been taught to eat whatever he got and not be picky. Putting another scrumptious pakora in his already salivating mouth, he decided that it would be a good idea to have a mid-evening nap. But he knew this idea was too good to be true, and that at any moment one of his friends would knock on his door. In weather like this, while Krish liked to cosy-up with some girl in some secluded little corner, Kabir liked to jog or wrestle or do whatever god knows these athletic-type nut jobs do.

Content with enjoying the present moment, he decided to

enjoy it while it lasted and closed his eyes. And lo, just as he had predicted, he heard the slish-slosh of wet footsteps, which he was sure were Kabir's (although praying to his gods that it wasn't) returning from his rain-storming, approaching his room. Samrat mentally searched the dump that he called his room, and tried to locate the object of Kabir's impending need, a towel.

'Hey Dholki! Open the door!' came a whisper which would have been inaudible had Samrat not been listening for it. He got up and grabbed a towel to salvage his room from the impending flood that Kabir's feet would bring in, and opened the door.

But Samrat was surprised to see that it was Krish. Krish was so wet that he could have passed off as a rain god himself. Samrat backed up immediately, forgetting the towel in his hand and the little wading pool caused by Krish. 'What the hell is wrong with you Krish, have you seen the weather outside? I thought it was Kabir returning from one of his maniac runs. What were you even doing outside in the rain? And why the hell were you just whispering?'

Krish splashed in hurriedly, carrying his waterproof Woodland bag, which finally seemed to have served its purpose, and placed it on the bed.

'Hey! Do you want my whole room to get wet?' Samrat complained, picking up the bag hurriedly, which clanged loudly as if it held something fragile and heavy.

'Oye! Careful with that! Do you know how much it is worth?' exclaimed Krish, reaching out for the bag.

'Yeah, yeah! I know it's very expensive, but why isn't it being expensive in your own room?' Samrat said, handing it over to Krish.

With his most mischievous grin, Krish gestured to Samrat

to come closer, and when he didn't budge but wore the same sulky expression, Krish came forward with a lunge and opened the bag ever so slightly and asked him to peer in.

Samrat peeped in, sceptical, thinking that this was another of Krish's pranks. However, once he did, he kept staring at the contents of the bag for two whole minutes and exclaimed 'Krish, what is all this for? Who is this for? Is your dad coming? Is it a gift for some professor? C'mon! Will you stop grinning and tell me already?'

'It's for us. Who else? Have you seen the weather? It comes once a year so we need to celebrate besides who knows where we will be next year?' Krish said, putting the bag to one side and taking out a bottle.

Samrat tried to suppress his grin as Krish posed like a bimbo in a wet shirt advertising cheap liquor. Instead, he said, 'Who's us? Because Dorky's not here and Kabir's running circles god knows where.'

'You know he should really call it swimming in this weather. I swear, sometimes I think he comes from a different planet. Anyway, let's just wait for him, he's bound to run into the danger of drowning soon, and then he will have to come in,' Krish chuckled.

Just then, Samrat's door flew open and Kabir came in pouring water everywhere. He said, 'Oh man, the rain is fierce today. I thought I would drown if I lost my balance. Hey Dholki, you wouldn't have a towel, would you?'

'Argh, why can't you guys just go to your own rooms? Don't you have towels there?' Samrat pulled out another towel from his cupboard and threw it at Kabir grumbling. 'Aww, because we love you Dholki, and we can't stay away from you,' Kabir teased while making kissing noises.

'Okay, so as I was explaining to Dholki, we are drinking tonight. And this isn't "invite everyone and party" drinking, it's more like "beautiful weather and we don't know where we will be next year" drinking,' Krish said to Kabir who was busy trying to get water out of his ear. Krish snapped, 'Hey, are you listening?'

'Yeah, I get it, just give me five minutes to freshen up,' he said, drying himself. Samrat couldn't resist taking a jab, 'You need five minutes? I thought you already took a shower outside, so all you need is a change of clothes.' Kabir smirked and threw the wet towel in Samrat's face and ran out of the room while Samrat detangled himself.

'So, why don't you guys give me ten minutes and then come to my room, then we can have some fun,' Krish said hurrying out.

As promised, Kabir walked towards Krish's room, all dry and freshened up, just as Samrat reached the door in exactly ten minutes. As they entered his room, Samrat saw that Krish had gone out of his way to make this night the perfect one—he had bought innumerable nibbles, and for some reason, he had put on old songs which he hated.

'Wow, food!' exclaimed the ever-hungry Kabir, rushing forward and grabbing a plate-full of snacks. Samrat jumped and snatched it away, saying, 'Hey! Easy with the munching, hulk, it's for all of us and should last as long as the drinks do; it's not for you alone.'

'Actually, this one is for him. Being the demon that he is, I knew he would be vastly hungry after his run, so I bought loads of extra food. So just chill Dholki, and for once let me take care of everything,' Krish said, taking the plate away from Samrat and handing it back to Kabir, who immediately put a chicken nugget in his salivating mouth.

Once they sat down and gulped down a couple of drinks like there was no tomorrow, Krish exclaimed, 'Slow and steady, guys. This is not a sprint but an all-night marathon.' All of them looked at each other, nodded, and then started to sip the drink in their hands slowly, a pace which lasted pretty much for exactly that one drink, after which they were back to drinking with their previous gusto.

Kabir, who at this point was intoxicated beyond belief, put his head between his knees and started to rock back and forth. Samrat and Krish, equally drunk, stumbled to his side thinking that he was going to puke any second, and rubbed his back vigorously. Krish brought a bucket and kept it in front of Kabir, who jerked his head up and said, 'What the hell are you guys doing?'

'We thought you were gonna puke. Aren't you?' Samrat asked confused, still swaying.

'No. So will you both quit rubbing my back,' Kabir snapped, irritated.

Samrat and Krish withdrew their hands immediately and wondered what they should do next: should they stand by his side or sit down? Finally, after what seemed like an eternity of awkwardness, they decided to sit down again and enjoy the evening. Krish hastily gulped down the rest of his glass. Re-energized for combat, he gave Kabir a hard stare and asked, 'Yaar, why do you always get so sad after drinking lately? I have noticed it a couple of times. I swear, sometimes I think you're turning into a chick. That's exactly what happens when your best friend is a girl.'

'Just shut up, Krish. I am in no mood for your jokes,' Kabir said, angry.

'See, so touchy he has become lately. What, are you getting your period or something?' Krish said, still smirking.

Aggravated, Kabir tried to get up, as though to punch Krish but slumped back again. Samrat, sensing the danger, got up and said, 'Krish, shut up, yaar. And Kabir, don't pay attention to him, just calm down. You know it's just us friends here. Had it been any other night I would have refereed this fight myself, but c'mon guys, there's good booze on the table. Just calm down and let me make you another drink, okay?'

Once Kabir had calmed down, Samrat handed him his drink and sat beside him. Carefully, as if treading on eggshells, he asked, 'Kabir, don't take it otherwise—but both of us have noticed that there is something on your mind bothering you. What's wrong? We just want you to be fine.'

Kabir looked at Samrat with pained eyes and opened his mouth to say something, but no sound came out. Samrat, guessing that he needed just a little bit of nudging, slurred calmly, 'See, Kabir. We just want you to be okay. It saddens us to see you upset, and I know that Krish feels the same way even if his actions seem otherwise.'

Kabir immediately grabbed his hair and howled, 'I can't stand it anymore. I can't breathe or sleep, I have even lost my appetite.' Samrat nodded understandingly and looked at all the empty plates in front him. 'No matter how much I try, I can't get over her.'

'Who?' asked Krish and Samrat, in unison.

'Mahi,' Kabir said, averting their eyes.

'What?' Samrat asked, baffled.

Krish looked as if someone had just handed him a treasure chest. He nudged Samrat and said, 'See, I told you he liked her.

I knew it, nobody spends that much time with a girl and not be in love or something.'

Kabir gave them both a hopeless look and slouched. Samrat put up a hand to quieten Krish, and slurred in between hiccups, 'Kabir, both of us had an inkling. But we didn't want to butt in, we thought you would tell us when you were ready.' Kabir looked at them wondering why he hadn't talked to them about it before, and gave them a smile which looked more like a grimace.

'So, what's the problem, go and tell her,' Krish said, suddenly butting in.

'It's not so simple. She's going out with Sidharth now,' Kabir said sadly.

'So, that's not permanent—Mahi goes out with lots of boys—it doesn't mean anything,' Krish said waving his hand as if flicking the imaginary boy away. 'Besides, with you it's going to be different. I don't really want to hear anything, tell her!' Krish said with such force that Kabir and Samrat both stared at him for a minute.

'C'mon man, do it. Do it now,' Krish said, thrusting his cell phone into Kabir's hand.

'On the phone, wow, that's romantic,' Kabir said sarcastically.

'Kabir, do you have the courage to do it to her face?' Krish asked, trying to reason with him.

'Hey, I have been looking for the perfect moment, I just never got the chance,' Kabir said, defending himself.

Krish chuckled and said, 'Yeah right, because you have been hanging out with her for what... over two and a half years now and you never found your chance. Hello, wake up and smell the coffee. Samrat, say something!'

Samrat put up his hands and crawled upto the foot of the

bed indicating that he wasn't a part of this conversation. Krish threw Kabir his cell phone once again, who sighed, giving in. He stared at the phone in his hand and suddenly got up saying, 'Fine, I will call her right now, but from my cell phone, not yours. God only knows how many girls will disturb the call in between if I use your phone.'

'Fine. Call her from your cell. Where is it?' Krish asked, looking around.

'It's in my room, I'll go get it,' Kabir said, trying to walk while holding on to the wall for support.

'No way... we may be drunk, but I know your plan. You think you can go into your room and lock us out and not make the call. Well, I am not falling for that one. Tell me where it is and I will get it for you,' Krish said, swaying dangerously.

Kabir gave him a long hard stare and then slid down the wall giving up. Finally, he said, 'It's on my bed.'

Samrat watched as Krish walked out of the room, and turned towards Kabir to say something encouraging. Kabir looked like he was going to throw up. Just as he was about to walk up to his friend and put his hand on his shoulder, Krish peered in and said, 'Um, Dholki. I can't find the phone, will you help me look for it?' Samrat looked at Kabir, who had turned to stone, and walked out of the room.

Once outside, he saw that Krish was brimming with mischief and asked him suspiciously, 'What are you doing?'

Krish, who was positively giddy with excitement, exclaimed as they walked towards Kabir's room, 'This is going to be the best night ever! Just wait and watch.'

Samrat sceptically followed Krish, still confused. When he saw Tanmay leaning on Kabir's door with his eyes closed, he asked

Krish, 'What's Tanmay doing here? What's wrong with him?'

'Nothing, he is hammered and he is looking for the loo,' Krish said, raising his eyebrows mischievously.

Understanding his intentions at once, Samrat looked flabbergasted. 'Are you crazy? Kabir is waiting for the phone to call Mahi. We can't do this, he will kill us.'

'Oh please, he will never know that it was us who did it. As for him calling Mahi, a) he isn't going to call, he is just making excuses, b) even if he does, do you really think drunk calling her is a good idea, and c) this will be so much fun!' Krish finished the list and moved ahead even before Samrat could comprehend it completely.

Krish walked to Tanmay and slapped him on the face. Tanmay opened his eyes and began shouting, 'What the hell? Why did you slap me?'

Krish smiled at him and said, 'There was a mosquito. I was saving you from malaria and god knows what other diseases. It is no point thinking about anyone else Samrat, we should have let it bite him.'

Tanmay became deeply distressed and hugged Krish while tears rolled down his cheeks. 'I am so sorry, Krish. You are my brother. How could I ever doubt you? I am so sorry. Look, I will lie at your feet but just forgive me.' Tanmay started to bend down, and Krish and Samrat managed to catch him before he toppled over.

'Arrey yaar, no problem. What are such little things between brothers? Don't worry about it. Weren't you looking for the loo? Let me take you there,' Krish exclaimed, extracting his arm from Tanmay, and pushing him into Kabir's room, which was pitch dark.

'Why is it so dark in here? Where are the lights?' Tanmay asked, stumbling into the room.

'The lights just went out. Don't worry, we are right here. Can you see the light coming from the window? There's the urinal,' Krish said while Samrat sniggered.

Tanmay unzipped and peed around the window while saying, 'Thank you so much guys. You are the best, I swear. I would have peed there in the hall if you hadn't helped me. Thank you so much.'

Just then a voice boomed, and both Samrat and Krish froze. 'What's going on here?' Kabir crossed the hall, peered in his room, and asked, 'Didn't you guys find my cell? What's wrong with you people? How drunk are you?'

Just then Tanmay walked out of the room, zipping up his pants, and said, 'Hey, Kabir. What's up, man?' Kabir looked at Tanmay, and caught hold of his shirt, 'What the hell were you doing in my room?'

Tanmay shook like a rag doll in Kabir's hands. 'Your room? no, wait, let me explain...' he said and slumped against Kabir's chest, passed out.

Samrat and Krish looked at the duo and heaved a sigh of relief as Kabir put Tanmay down on the ground in disgust and walked into his room. Thirty seconds later, Kabir walked out of the room, his face purple, and yelled so loudly that every other student came out of their rooms, 'Son of a bitch, he peed in my room!'

As everyone took turns to peep inside Kabir's room, and Kabir rumbled on calling for wardens and teachers, Samrat leaned in and said to Krish, 'You were right—Best Night Ever!'

≈

5

In the Light of New Evidence

'YOU GUYS MUST be careful about who you drink with, or at least make sure to point this guy in the right direction,' Kabir said, walking in, taking a jab at Tanmay.

'Look who's here finally. What took you so long? Did your invitation have a different time printed on it, or did Mr Bigshot Lawyer forget the way to our meagre little college?' Krish teased as he gave Kabir a huge hug. 'And you aren't still mad about that little incident, are you? C'mon Kabir, it was a long time ago… and I don't think we need to worry about that tonight since none of us own a room here,' Krish said, trying to hide his grin behind his glass.

'Yes, but you do have a car, don't you, maybe he can use that today,' Kabir snickered while nudging Samrat, who spurted alcohol, coughed, and laughed at the same time.

'Hey, I am right here, in case I wore my invisibility suit today,' grumbled Tanmay.

Losing interest in the conversation, Krish looked around to see if there was any sign of Akshii, who as usual was not picking up her phone. Of course, they all knew when Mahi would arrive. Although he loved both the girls equally, he had a soft corner for Akshii. After all, only he knew what was under that hard exterior. He had always known that Akshii was a fighter, which probably came from being the middle child. He had never understood her relationship with her parents and siblings though. She said it wasn't anything special, but he couldn't make sense of how anyone who had grown up in a house with two parents and two siblings could resent their family so much.

Whenever he had asked, she had said that she'll tell him when the time was right, but she had never told him. Ever since they had formed the group they had been inseparable, and why not, Akshii was more a boy than him or Kabir at some things. Although everybody in college had thought at one point of time or the other that there was something going on between them, those rumours remained just rumours. In fact, truth be told, she was more like a sister he had never had. He owed his degree to her since she had almost carried him through their college years. While everyone rightly thought that Mahi was the life of their little group, Akshii was the glue that held them together all those years. She just knew exactly what they wanted or even needed to hear, knew exactly how to motivate them, aggravate them and also how to pacify each one of them.

'Where are you off to? Hello, earth to Krish,' Kabir nudged him, interrupting his thoughts.

He smiled at his friends and said, 'Just thinking about the good old days. I mean those were the days, man.' Kabir laughed suddenly, 'Remember when that construction work was going on in campus, and Banerjee fell into that small hole and started to scream saying that he doesn't want to die.'

All of them laughed loudly at the memory, and once they did, the memories seemed endless. 'Yeah, the amount he prayed to Kali Mata, I wouldn't be surprised if she actually got irritated and pushed him down that hole.'

'Well! He did have his share of bad luck. Remember when Gaurav came back late that night and someone convinced him that Banerjee had resigned and was leaving the very next morning? Oh man, I can't believe that he went and told him to suck it!' Tanmay exclaimed.

'Remember it? I know who convinced him! It was definitely the best night ever,' Kabir said, grinning.

'Who, who, who... c'mon tell me whoooo!' Tanmay tugged on Kabir's sleeve.

'Stop making sounds like an owl, man. Just guess... who has such a devious mind? I mean, whose sole purpose in college was to create ripples in everyone else's life?' Kabir answered, pointing towards...

'Krish!' Tanmay exclaimed.

'Yeah?' Krish answered, turning around as he heard his name.

'It was you... all these years I kept wondering who could have done something like that. Nobody even guessed. I am sure you must have had a good laugh at another's expense... heck everyone did,' Tanmay exclaimed.

'What are we talking about?' Krish asked sceptically, as Samrat's heartbeat rose steadily.

'You know what we are talking about. We finally figured out who created so much trouble all those years ago,' Kabir said, giving him a cold stare, trying very hard not to laugh.

'Oh, crap! You know...? How? We never told anybody! How

the heck did you remember, you were so drunk we figured you wouldn't remember, ever. Kabir, man, we were so stupid, you know that, and we just wanted to have some fun that night. So, so drunk,' Krish said stepping away from him slowly.

'And don't forget so drunk! Kabir, please yaar, it was ages ago, you can't possibly be mad about it still,' Samrat chipped in from the side.

'What are you guys...?' Tanmay tried to speak, confusion etched on his face, but was shushed by Kabir.

'Well, I am still mad about it,' Kabir said, although he had no idea what they were talking about. Right now, all he knew was that he wanted to get to the bottom of this thing that he wasn't supposed to be mad about.

'C'mon man, it was just a stupid prank, it didn't really mean anything,' Krish said, gulping as Kabir towered in front of him ready to charge.

'Oh, as opposed to all your other pranks which, of course, were aimed at world destruction?' Kabir smirked.

'That's not what I meant, you know that! All I meant was that it was so obvious, and so easy, we just had to do it. And it didn't hurt anyone. Besides, you did make a fool of me on the football field just the day before. I forgave you. Be the bigger man. Back me up here, Samrat,' Krish said, trying to back away slowly.

'Oh yeah, absolutely. Besides, I just want to add, Kabir, it was all Krish's idea. Entirely his. I kept saying no, but he wouldn't listen. You know how he is. He never listens to anyone. He saw Tanmay who was looking for the loo, and he steered him into your room,' Samrat said, trying to hide his grin, loving the fact that it was his friend who was on the receiving end for a change.

Krish looked at Samrat aghast; his friend had just thrown him under the bus with no remorse. He immediately turned to Kabir who stood there unresponsive with his mouth open.

Tanmay, on the other hand, erupted like a volcano, 'You did that! Oh my god, Krish, how could you? Do you know what I went through all these years? That's why everyone still calls me Tinkle Fairy!'

Krish doubled over and pressed his stomach as if he was in pain, but both Kabir and Samrat knew that he was struggling to maintain a straight face. He finally took a deep breath and looked at both Kabir and Tanmay's faces. 'Wait, you guys didn't know about this? We thought you had figured it out. Then what were you so angry about?'

'We were fishing, I got suspicious when you said "are you still angry about it",' Kabir said, rubbing his knuckles.

Krish looked at them with a sheepish grin and said, 'See, I am so, so sorry. Tanmay, please listen. C'mon, it was just a prank.'

'You know what Krish, suck this,' Tanmay grimaced, walking away and pointing towards a part of his anatomy.

'Tanmay, c'mon,' Krish said apologetically, while Tanmay made a rude hand gesture from all the way across the room.

Looking at his friend who couldn't stop laughing, Kabir wondered how ten long years had passed since they had graduated, but to him, it felt just like yesterday. But as he looked around, he realized that the years had left their mark on so many known faces.

He saw how the faces of the women Krish had once dated were now lined with worry and motherhood, and how the guys with whom he had once competed had lost their races to receding hair lines and paunchy tummies. He looked at himself and wondered if he had lost the race too. However, Lady Health seemed to like him, and he felt as fit as he did in his college days.

Kabir looked at the sea of faces, and decided to let bygones be bygones. *'Have so many things changed since college?'* he asked himself. *'Well maybe, for other people,'* he thought. *'But somehow my life has stood still since that night.'*

Kabir did not know whether to hate that night or just be thankful that it happened. Granted that people may call it foolish, heck, he himself would call it foolish, but the heart yearns for what the heart yearns.

And his mind wandered to that night when his life became stagnant.

6

Time Wrap

KABIR HAD ALWAYS believed that feelings like 'butterflies in the tummy' and 'music in one's ears' were just phrases thrown into sappy romances which sold only because of delusional girls. Least of all he never imagined that something like this would happen to him, never had he imagined that he would fall in love at first sight, or end up being the best friend to the same girl, or even struggle to tell her that he loved her. But he decided that today would be the day it was all going to change. With that thought in his mind, his heart skipped a beat and he couldn't help but smile infectiously. As he hummed his favourite tune, he reached his room and put all the food on the table. Since Mahi had accepted his invitation to have dinner with him, he had literally turned insomniac. Although they had been to dinner numerous times, sometimes with the rest of their friends and sometimes just both of them, this one was pretty special, at least for him. It was her birthday and he wanted it to be perfect. He had stayed up all night making a list of all the food she liked, and had made a playlist of all her favourite songs.

Then, in the morning, he had rushed to all the restaurants on the list, just so that he could have everything ready. Of course he had to wait, some of them hadn't even opened yet, but he didn't mind, he didn't mind anything today.

Although dinner was supposed to be at eight o' clock, he went down and started decorating at six. He knew Mahi loved candles and her favourite flower was rajnigandha, and even though she told everybody that she loved roses, he knew. He went down to the morning flower market, as he was on a budget, and bought the candles and flowers. As he started decorating, he realized that he didn't know what to say to her. He wished that he could just talk to Krish or Samrat or Akshii about it, but all of them had gone back home for the Christmas vacation. It had been a stroke of luck that the both of them had to stay back for a few days. Actually, it was Mahi who had had to stay back, but as soon as he knew she wasn't leaving, he wasn't either.

Taking a deep breath, he decided he would just have to go with the flow. By the time he finished decorating, he only had half an hour to get ready. He rushed back to the room, he knew Mahi hated waiting. He didn't want to spoil the evening by making her wait, so he just took a cold shower and wore his shirt and leather jacket without bothering to dry off.

At precisely five minutes to eight, Kabir stood in front of the hostel gates. As each minute passed, his anxiety increased by leaps and bounds; each minute felt like a year. And then, he saw her. Although she wore a simple pair of jeans and a plain pink sweater and very little make-up, to Kabir she looked as if she was dressed in the world's most beautiful dress. For a minute, while she walked towards him, Kabir literally forgot to breathe. She smiled as she reached him and said, 'Hi! Chilly, no?'

As if woken up from a trance, he hugged her and wished her, 'Hi. Happy birthday! You look beautiful, as usual.'

'Thank you. So, where are we going?' Mahi asked smiling. 'The mess?'

Kabir shook his head and smiled mysteriously. 'It's a surprise. So you will have to wait just a little while more.'

'What does a little while mean, Kabir? I'm starving,' Mahi asked pouting.

'Fine, then let's just get started.' Kabir smiled as he pulled out a scarf from his pocket and started to fold it into a blindfold.

'What...are you...doing? I am not wearing that,' Mahi said sceptically.

'Oh c'mon Mahi, it's just for a little while, please, and it's part of a surprise. Don't spoil it. Please.' Kabir made sad eyes at her.

'Okay fine! But, only for a little while. It's going to spoil my mascara.'

Kabir laughed and started to blindfold her. As he guided her towards his bike, he felt her lean on him for support and his heart raced. The December wind blew, making the evening chilly, and her hair brushed his face. For a minute he forgot where they were going, and he just breathed in the fragrance of her shampoo. Although he wished he could do just this his whole life, he snapped back to reality as they reached his bike.

'Okay, now can you sit on the bike without looking, or should I open it?' Kabir asked.

'If I say no, will you take this stupid thing off my eyes?' Mahi asked, but smiled immediately and said, 'I am fine. Don't worry.'

With that she climbed up, feeling her way, and grabbed his shoulders for support. As Kabir started, he felt Mahi's grip tighten, and he smiled. 'Mahi, relax, I'm not going to let you fall, trust me okay.'

'Well, I'd relax if only you'd tell me where we are going, and then you wouldn't have to put this irritating thing on my eyes,' Mahi grimaced.

Kabir laughed and said, 'Patience, Mahi, is a virtue. And besides, it's not very far; just wait for a little while more.'

'We've been on the road for only two or three minutes. According to my calculations, we're not even in the city yet. Where are we going, Kabir?' He stopped the bike abruptly.

'That's because we are not going into the city, we are going someplace special,' Kabir said, helping her get off the bike. As they reached the main gate, he took off Mahi's blindfold and held his breath, waiting for her reaction.

As expected, Mahi's face fell as she gazed upon 'Kabir's Special Place', which happened to be their college's pet dhaba, just half a kilometre away from their campus. She pouted, 'Here? Don't get me wrong, Kabir, I have no problem with it. In fact, I love it. It's just that you said we were going somewhere special. In fact, I don't get why you blindfolded me. We could have walked till here, it's practically right in front of our college.'

Kabir smiled and led her inside, 'Mahi, all that glitters is not gold, you know. Besides, haven't you ever heard that good things come in small packages? Just wait and watch.'

Mahi smiled and nudged him, 'Wow! Someone's been taking philosophy lessons. All right Mr Hotshot, blow me away.'

When they reached the terrace it was pitch black, but the sweet fragrance of rajnigandha whiffed through the air. He led her to the middle of the terrace, and then switched on the fairy lights he had made them put up. As soon as he flipped the switch, the whole terrace glittered with hundreds of small shimmering lights, but Kabir had eyes only for the glow which lit Mahi's face.

While she stood overwhelmed, Kabir got busy lighting the candles. Mahi looked around and spoke with delight in her voice, 'Oh my god! How did you manage to do this? This is the best birthday ever, Kabir. Thanks! I have no words. But you have to tell me how you got this done...?'

'Oh, well! A little bit of talk here and there, and you know, it just fell in place. So anyway, let's get started. My lady!' Kabir bowed down with his hand stretched out to her.

Mahi instantly grabbed it and rushed forward to give him a hug. She whispered in his ear, 'Thank you, it's perfect.'

'I am glad you like it,' Kabir said sheepishly.

'Like it? Are you mad? I love it. Come, let's sit down.' As she sat down on the floor where he had spread out a mattress and a sheet, Kabir brought out plastic cups and a bottle of wine in his hand.

'Oh my god, Kabir you shouldn't have. This is very expensive. I would have been okay drinking something else,' Mahi exclaimed looking at the label.

'I know you would have been fine, but this is your favourite, isn't it?' Kabir said, handing her a glass. 'Now, will you please relax and not worry about how expensive it is. I will get the food in the meanwhile.'

As he heated up the food and plated it as beautifully as his testosterone allowed him, he watched Mahi look up at the stars and smiled at her. If only he could just breathe in this moment. Once they were finished with their meal and a whole lot of wine, Kabir finally mustered up the courage to go ahead with his plan. As he started to speak up, Mahi pulled out her phone which was silently buzzing away to glory and said, 'It's Sidharth. Do you mind if I take it?' Kabir shook his head and tried to calm himself down, thinking that he had waited for two and a half years, how long could a damn phone call be? But that's where he was wrong, because that phone call seemed to last his whole life.

As Mahi put the phone down, Kabir's spirits soared again and he mentally prepared himself as he thought that it was now or never. So deciding that it had to be now, he started to position himself on his knee, thinking it may help as it was the oldest trick in romance movies. Mahi turned towards him with a wide smile on her face and laughed suddenly as she saw Kabir. 'What are you doing Kabir? Are you looking for something?'

Abashed, Kabir gulped and spoke 'Uh... Mahi...well, I just... Ah...I actually...Umm. You and me...you know...I wanted you to know that...umm.' However, by the clearly confused look on Mahi's face he knew he was royally screwing up and so taking a deep breath he decided to just blurt it out. But even before he could, Mahi chimed in, 'Anyway, tell me later. Sidharth is on his way. He flew all the way here so that I wouldn't be alone on my birthday. Isn't it sweet? So, as he is already reaching college, I just told him to come here. Oh, I am so excited, and you can also meet him finally. Kabir, say something.'

'Huh, yeah...yeah I would love to. I mean yes I would like to meet him.' Kabir spoke, still trying to comprehend the whole situation. And even before he could, Mahi's phone vibrated again and she picked it up with lighting speed and spoke, 'Are you here already? Yes, I am celebrating my birthday here. C'mon, you will like it once you come up here.'

She swooned as she waited for him, which wasn't very long. Sidharth walked in dressed in suave designer clothes carrying the largest bouquet of long-stemmed pristine red roses Kabir had ever seen. His heart sank as he saw Mahi run over and give Sidharth a hug. As they broke apart, Sidharth handed over the bouquet to Mahi and waved Kabir over giving him a cursory smile. 'Kabir, right? Good to see you, man. Mahi talks about all of you so much, its like I practically know you. Hey, listen, thanks for everything, man. I had planned for a whole day but some important meetings came up. I was devastated that her birthday would be ruined but you saved the day, bro.' Sidharth ranted in a voice laced with a thick accent. Kabir tried to speak but then settled for a polite smile.

'I mean look at this place. WOW. Actually to tell you the truth when Mahi told me where to come and I reached downstairs, the first thing that crossed my mind was why is Mahi spending her birthday here, in this dump? So I hope you don't mind I asked the concierge of my hotel to pack up a basket of food and wine and send it over. Besides it's a very special day. It's Mahi's birthday and she deserves only the best of the best. Don't you agree, Kabir?' he spoke glancing at the bottle of wine on the floor.

'Hey, that's my favourite wine.' Mahi said as she playfully punched Sidharth's arm. 'Oh I am sure it is, my love. And rightly so it is a good bottle of wine but it's not the best. And you deserve only the best.' Sidharth spoke quickly.

'But Kabir bought it especially for my birthday, Sidharth,' Mahi spoke keeping in mind the effort Kabir had made for the day.

'It's really no big deal, Mahi.' Kabir said understanding her predicament. 'Besides he is right, you deserve only the best of the best.'

Before Mahi could put up another argument, Sidharth spoke 'Guys, it's okay. Infact, I have an idea. I was actually going to wait till everything arrived, thought it would make it really special but I guess this is already quite special and close to Mahi's heart. So, why don't we toast with this one here and then celebrate with the other one later. What say Kabir?'

Kabir nodded, as he was still lost for words. He was sure that they could practically hear his heart which was thumping extra hard. Ironically, his head, on the other hand, had decided to shut down completely and for the first time in his life he felt as if he was moving in a trance. He had heard the stories when people said they had an out of body experience but this was the first time he was experiencing something of the sort.

Unattached, he watched without any emotion as Sidharth bent down on his knee and brought out a green box with Tiffany and Co embossed on it. Kabir looked on—he could see Sidharth's lips move but couldn't hear anything. However, he didn't really need to hear to comprehend anymore. Mahi's expression, as Sidharth slid a beautiful large blue diamond ring on her finger, was enough to snap Kabir back to reality.

While they hugged and kissed Kabir quietly slid down from the terrace and started walking down the road without looking back.

≈

7

The Queen Descends

'TAKE THE THIRD left from the main road, another left from the T-junction, and then just follow the road to the end.' As Mahi gave directions to the chauffeur, she grew more annoyed that she even had to. She sat back, pondering whether she should just ask the chauffeur to drop her back at the hotel. Her life had turned into a nightmare in the last ten years. Her eyes started to well up at the thought, but she quelled the tears so that it would not spoil her mascara. She retrieved a dainty lace handkerchief from her one-of-a-kind designer clutch and dried her eyes. After all, Mahi Shah wasn't anything if not just perfect. With that thought, she started to smoothen out the imaginary wrinkles on the beautiful red dress her husband had gifted her. Like everything else she owned, it was designed specifically for her. Looking at her one-of-a-kind dress, she started to think about her one-of-a-kind life, and a series of recent events trailed in front of her mind's eye.

However, she was heaved into the immediacy of the moment when the car door opened suddenly. 'Ma'am, we have arrived. Do you need a minute before stepping out?' the chauffeur asked.

'No, I'm perfect,' Mahi said, stepping out with her best foot forward and the smile she had perfected over the years.

As she wafted through the corridors, she realized that she had butterflies in her stomach. She smiled at the thought that even after all these years, something like this could make her nervous. Strangely happy to realize that she could still feel something, anything at all, she walked in with a new spring in her step as she saw Krish acroos the ballroom.

'Aren't we too old for this, Mahi? You really should stop your childish games. It's been ten years now,' Krish chuckled with pseudo-annoyance as Mahi covered his eyes from behind. Truth be told, whenever she was around, he was both a kid and a big brother. Although he had never felt attraction towards her the way the other boys had, he had always felt protective of her. For some reason she had always seemed a fragile doll to him, even though she used every ounce of her energy to play the role of a full-blown bitch. While she kept up a hard exterior to the world, inside she was quite vulnerable.

'Hello, my angel! How have you been? Where is everybody else... where's Akshii, shouldn't she be here by now? Can you believe it's been ten years since we left college? Why aren't you saying anything?' Mahi spoke continuously in one breath.

Krish looked at her amazed and finally spoke, 'How can you still speak so fast, Mahi? Breathe please, or else you will turn a shade darker than your dress.'

'Oh! You like it? It's Elise Berrien you know, one-of-a-kind,' Mahi chirped.

'It's nice, but why would you spend so much on a dress?'

Krish interjected, looking at her from top to toe and realizing that Mahi was living the dream she had always wanted.

'Um... perhaps the same reason, that you spend ten times more on that car I saw outside. Yes, I knew that was yours,' she retorted affectionately. As he had predicted, every eye in the room followed her. He saw how every guy looked at her with reverence, and how the looks she got from all the girls were the exact opposite. 'Hey, just so you know, your life may be in danger tonight. These girls might just rip your throat out. I mean, look at you, you haven't aged a day. What's your secret? Plastic surgery, yoga, donkey milk or bathing in chicken blood?' Krish snickered.

Mahi laughed, infectiously, and asked again, 'Where is everyone?'

'Oh well, you know Akshii isn't here yet. Kabir and Samrat have been gulping down their drinks, so they have gone to get refills.' Krish spoke as he considered getting his own as well, when he saw Kabir and Samrat returning, laughing.

'Mahi! When did you get here? My, my, don't you look awesome,' Samrat said pecking her on the cheek. 'Doesn't she look amazing, Kabir? Dressed all in red... don't you think she looks like a dream come true?' Samrat said giving him a knowing smile.

Kabir gave him a look which made it clear that he was going to kill Samrat as soon as Mahi looked the other way. He turned around, smiled at Mahi and gave her a hug, 'Hi, how are you, Mahi? As already pointed out, you look lovely tonight, as always.'

Mahi looked into Kabir's eyes as if searching for something, and then turned away with a pained expression. She struggled to find something else to talk about, and finally said, 'Isn't this event supposed to be catered, or did they forget to hire servers? Anyway, I need a drink, so can someone point me towards a bar?'

'Wow, Mahi getting her own drink, that has to be a first. Are you sure you don't want to bat your eyelashes at some poor soul?' Krish elbowed her, smirking. 'Relax, princess! I'm just joking. Don't hurt your pretty little feet, I'll get you your drink. What'll you like?' Krish said, gesturing to the waitress, who was waiting for his signal.

'Can I help you, Sir?' said the waitress with a sugar-dipped smile. 'Can you get me my usual, and a glass of red wine for the lady, sweetheart?' Krish said with a smile.

'Certainly, Sir,' the waitress said excusing herself.

As she walked away, both Kabir and Samrat looked at Krish incredulously, 'Where the hell was she when we were getting our elbows bruised on our way to the bar?'

'Hey, you never asked. And I can't let a lady get her own drink. I have a reputation to maintain after all,' Krish said smirking.

As they all jibber-jabbered with each other, Mahi couldn't help but realize how light-hearted she was feeling. It was as if the last ten years hadn't happened at all. She felt like a college kid again, filled with all kinds of hopes and dreams. After a very long time, she could once again believe that in the end, everything would turn out to be all right. And in that moment, she began to remember her favourite night in all her college years.

≈

8

Ice Princess

IT HAD BEEN a frantic day in the girl's hostel. There was utter chaos everywhere. Everybody seemed to be running around as though there was a fire blazing somewhere. Today was the fresher's party, and every girl was vying for the crown which was to be given out at the end of the party.

Although the event was five hours away, preparations had been put in motion since the week had started. After all, there was a lot to be done and getting dressed perfectly for a party was not a joke. Amidst all the commotion breaking out in the washroom, Mahi rushed out from the shower, soaking wet, and scuttled towards her room at the end of the corridor, wrapped in a soaking wet tiny silk bathrobe.

Since the party had been announced, Mahi had taken it upon herself to hand out fashion advice to everyone. Almost everybody ran their wardrobe by her, be it a pair of earrings, or the perfect pair of heels. For days her closet had been cleaned out, and Mahi was really proud of some of the outfits she had put together for some of the other girls. But no matter how much she tried, she just could not bend Kamakshii to her will.

Kamakshii, the college tomboy, had decided, to Mahi's utter distaste, that she was going to wear jeans and high tops to the party. As she had vowed to herself that she was not going to let that happen, Mahi had been scheming since the minute she had woken up to get Akshii into the dress that she had picked out for her.

As she entered the room, she saw Akshii lying down on the bed, eating a large bag of chips, and watching an episode of Friends. She couldn't stop herself from snapping exasperatedly, 'Akshii, what the hell is wrong with you, we just had lunch, and look at you! What in the world are you eating? You do know that's pure fat!'

She let out a couple of cleansing breaths, calmed herself down and started again, 'Anyway, why the hell are you lying down? And why in the world aren't you getting ready?'

Mahi lost her cool as Akshii went on eating chips, one after the other, paying no heed to her. She yanked the packet of chips out of Akshii's hands and threw it into the bin.

'Hey, what gives? Mahi, I was hungry. And that 'lunch' which you mentioned was all-salad, because god forbid if any girl on your table mentions bread or carbs, or worse butter!' Akshii got up irked.

'Oh please, you keep eating like this and pretty soon you'll need a table of your own because there won't be space for anyone else. How much do you eat, Akshii? God! I wish I had your metabolism,' Mahi retorted making a face.

'Oh yeah? It's called sports, you should try it sometime—it may just knock some sense into that fat-starved brain of yours.

Besides, the party happens to be at least five hours away!' Akshii yelled.

'Precisely, Akshii. It's only five hours away. Do you know how much work there is still to be done? The hair, the make-up, getting dressed, it's endless. And don't even get me started on you. I mean, who knows how much time it will take to transform this train wreck?' Mahi said, gesturing towards Akshii from head to toe.

Akshii looked at Mahi incredulously. 'Fine, considering you need to get a lot done, I will just get out of your way,' she said picking up her basketball.

'Uh-uh! Where do you think you are going?' Mahi asked blocking Akshii's way.

'Outside. Completely and totally away from you. So, if you just let me go now, I will no longer be in your hair,' Akshii retorted.

'Akshii, I haven't eaten anything cooked in two days. I am famished and that generally makes me crankier than usual. So trust me when I say I will physically hurt you if you do not start getting ready right about now,' Mahi threatened.

'Yeah, like that's ever gonna happen,' Akshii snorted while walking out.

'Okay, maybe that is never going to happen, but tell me, have you seen your photo album lately?' Mahi smiled viciously as Akshii stopped dead in her tracks. She knew that if nothing else, this would give her the leverage over Akshii. "God bless moms." She thought to herself and quickly flashed back to the day when Akshii's mom had got her an album of all the activities she had participated in as a child or rather was made to participate in. Although aunty had thought it would be a great gift for Akshii, she had hated them as much as she had hated the actual events whether it was a picture of her doing Bharatnatyam or an assortment of pictures where she was dressed in her older sister's clothes. And Mahi knew that she would hate for these pictures to be seen by anyone ever, even her best friends. Mahi had no intention of letting them see the pictures but as long as the threat holds, her life would be a lot easier.

'You wouldn't dare,' Akshii growled.

'Oh, sweetheart! You know me too well by now to know that I would,' Mahi smiled as Akshii tried frantically to find her album, tossing and turning everything in sight.

Finally, after almost forty-five minutes of searching and hollering, which ended with their room looking like a war zone and Mahi finishing up her nails outside, Akshii gave up. She slouched on her bed defeated and said grouchily, 'Fine, what do I have to do?'

Mahi got up, gave her a mawkish smile, and said, 'Okay, we have a lot to get done, so let's get started. First things first, go wash your hair, then we need to do your nails, and blow dry the hair. Some mousse should do the trick.'

'But I just washed my hair yesterday, and I really don't want any flashy colour on my fingers. Please. They look so girly, Mahi... all right, fine, I am going,' Akshii grumbled grabbing her bath essentials.

Mahi knew that Akshii wasn't like the other girls, she was very hard-core when it came to being as tomboyish as possible. So, of course, she hated all parties. In fact, her definition of styling her hair meant pulling it up into a ponytail. Mahi shuddered at the thought.

Now that there was the threat looming over her head,

Akshii put up a lot less resistance than Mahi had anticipated. She wilfully painted her fingers, blow-dried her hair, and got into the ultra-feminine baby pink dress that Mahi had picked out.

Once they were ready and done with their final touches, it was time to step into their heels. And as Akshii found it degrading to have a pair of heels in her closet, and she wasn't accustomed to stepping into someone else's shoes, this ultimately resulted in her wobbling down the corridor even before she could get to the stairs. After a quick practice run up and down the corridor, they finally decided to test the waters by taking on the stairs. By then, almost every girl on the floor was hurriedly floating towards the venue.

As they crossed the first flight of stairs, they heard a huge rip. For a second, it was as if all of them had turned into stone, and then all hell broke loose as all of them checked their attire in a quick frenzy. Suddenly, a quiet voice came from amidst them which timidly said, 'It's me.'

Mahi slumped as she recognized the voice. 'Akshii, what did you do?' she asked, sitting down to check the damage.

'I told you these heels were a bad idea. I guess now I can go and change into my jeans and high tops,' Akshii said with a hidden smile. But looking at her friend's dejected face she let out a sigh, and said, 'Can it be salvaged? I am pretty good with a needle and thread courtesy mom...'

'No, we don't have enough time for that,' Mahi said sadly.

'Mahi, I am really sorry. I swear I didn't do it on purpose. I will do anything, please don't be so sad,' Akshii said, trying to lift up her friend's spirits.

'I know you didn't do it on purpose... Did you actually mean it when you said that you would do anything?' Mahi asked, making her famous big eyes which always got the job done.

'Yeah, I guess. So, please stop looking at me like that,' Akshii said suspiciously, as she thought that fitting into a girly dress was the worst thing that could have happened to her, couldn't it? What more could happen?

'Okay come with me, I have an idea,' Mahi exclaimed smiling.

'But Mahi, you need to go and register for the pageant. They need you to be there in person or else they will not accept your form, and the registration is open only for another forty minutes or so,' whispered Sneha.

'I will make it, don't worry,' Mahi yelled, running up the stairs with Akshii. As soon as they reached their room, Mahi opened up her cupboard and started to throw all the clothes out. Finally, after ten minutes of frantic searching, she turned back to Akshii with what looked like something a little longer than a pink handkerchief in her hand.

'What the hell is that?' Akshii asked quizzically.

'It's a wrap!' Mahi exclaimed. 'C'mon Akshii,' she pleaded, 'It will just look like a short skirt, nobody is gonna know the difference. Just trust me please.'

Akshii, after giving Mahi a look as if she had asked for her first born, finally started to wrap it around her. Time flew in leaps and bounds while Mahi scrunched down and started to pin it together. 'Will you give me a hand down here? What're you doing? Are you playing a game?' Mahi asked angrily as Akshii was busy fiddling with her phone.

Finally, Mahi got up, touched-up her make-up and Akshii's, and said, 'Yeah, now you are ready to par-tay! Let's hurry and see if the registration for the crown is still on.'

They rushed down, but the desk at the side of the ground was already closed. Mahi slumped for a second when she saw the empty desk, but smiled when Akshii said dejectedly, 'Oh no, we missed it. I am so, so sorry, you missed it because of me.'

'Akshii, it's totally cool, it's just a crown and who cares. Hey, I don't need their seal of approval to tell me I'm hot and happening. I know that already, and you know it too,' Mahi said putting her brave face on.

'Hell! Everybody knows that, sweetie,' Krish quipped from behind. Once the five of them had gathered around, they forgot all about the crown, and got busy laughing and dancing. In fact, the pageant was the last thing on their minds and they didn't even remember it until they heard the announcement asking them to gather around.

Mahi's face fell and she said, 'Do we really have to stay here? Let's go, I'm starving.'

'You just ate, Mahi. What happened to your whole 'no-carbs' philosophy?' Akshii smiled. 'We can go in a minute, let's just hear the result. Pleaseeeee!'

The voice boomed over the microphone, making everyone look up. 'As all of us have been anticipating this very moment the whole evening, let's not dilly-dally anymore. I give you your princess: Miss Mahi...'

'What? How's that even possible? What did you do...?' Mahi blurted amidst claps.

'Well, let's just say I will have to date a couple of girls. You know, show them a good time. It's such a gigantic task. You owe me a huge one,' Krish chuckled.

≈

9

Den-Mother Speaks

A S AKSHII STEPPED in, her heart swelled at the sight of four of her favourite people. It had been a decade, but she knew that as soon as she sat down at that table, even if all of time came to a halt for another ten years, she still wouldn't be able to soak up enough of them.

Smiling at the thought, and with a skip in her step, she walked towards them. Each of them looked extremely happy. Almost tip-toeing to the table so that nobody would hear her, she playfully ruffled Krish's hair saying, 'Ew, Pretty Boy, how much product do you have in your hair. And, why?'

They got up to greet her, and Mahi's scream gave everyone else at the reunion an excuse to stare at them, which they were kind of doing already.

'Oh my god Mahi, you've made me deaf. Literally, there's buzzing in my ear. I can't decide on what to be more furious about, you making me deaf or Akshii spoiling my hair. I mean seriously, girls I know both of you can't really keep your hands off me but try at the least. After all, both of you are married,'

Krish said, nudging Kamakshii.

'You greeted him first—see, you proved that you love him more,' Mahi pouted.

'So, you wanted to get your hair ruffled too? Please by all means, love her more if that is what it takes to get you out of my hair, literally,' Krish chuckled with mock annoyance.

'I love all of you the same. C'mon guys, it's been ten years and you are still fighting about the same things! And Mahi, I would have ruffled your hair, but I don't have a death wish,' Akshii said hugging Samrat.

'Ahem, quick question. Were Samrat and I even in consideration?' Kabir asked, winking and giving Akshii a hug.

'Oh my god! Guys stop it! Let's just sit down now and catch up. I have so much to talk to you guys about! But first things first, I need some drinks, yes, as in plural. C'mon, Mama needs to have some fun tonight,' Akshii said smiling.

Once they were all settled down, they started to talk about their lives. Akshii passed around the photographs she had made her husband handpick from piles of family pictures. And after she had answered all their questions about her family, and had tucked away the pictures in her bag, she said, 'Okay, for tonight nobody's going to be a mom, wife, dad, C.E.O., or anything even remotely important or responsible. We are all getting drunk, and before anyone says anything, I am not taking no for an answer. And so help me god if you do, I am personally going to shove drinks down your throats.'

Mahi looked at Akshii positively beaming and said, 'Oh, looks like I have created a monster. But I say yes to an evening of inebriation. God knows I need to forget my life for the moment.'

All of them turned to look at Mahi, who beckoned the

waitress and ordered a round of shots. As she turned back to the table, she was taken aback by everybody's faces towards her. 'What?' she said, confused.

Akshii finally asked her, 'Mahi, is there something you want to discuss? Is everything all right?'

Mahi looked at her friends and said, 'Yeah, absolutely. Nothing serious. It's just that I had a tiff with Sidharth before leaving. But please, I just want to be with all of you today and not think about anybody else for now.'

Akshii, sensing that a change of topic was due, looked around and said, 'Hey, has anybody seen Dorky yet? Is he even coming tonight?'

'None of us have talked to him in ages. He just vanished after college—we tried everything, e-mails, messages, calling,' answered Samrat, shaking his head looking severely uncomfortable.

'What the hell happened between you guys? He literally disintegrated in front of our eyes. After that day he just changed—he showed up at the final exams completely drunk, and picked up fights in between the paper. I tried talking to him, but he just shoved me aside. Something else must have happened between you guys. Tell me, no?' Akshii asked, saddened at the thought of her missing friend.

'Nothing at all, you were there, he just yelled and walked away the day before our finals. We kept calling him even after we graduated, but he refused to talk to us after that day. Don't look at me like that, we all tried, but none of us got through to him. Besides, we never even knew what was wrong with him,' Kabir lied through his teeth hoping nobody would notice.

'Can we please talk about something else?' Mahi said, looking acutely uncomfortable.

'Mahi, what's wrong? Do you know something? Did you talk to him? Do you know where he is?' Akshii badgered on, knowing Mahi's expressions well.

'Oh my god, Akshii, will you please slow down? And no, I don't know anything about your precious Dorky. So, please stop looking at me like that,' Mahi said grimacing. 'Guys, c'mon. Stop it. I am serious. I don't know where he is, but I do know that he got fired some time back.'

'What? How in the world do you know this?' Kabir asked surprised.

'Sidharth has a friend who works in the same firm. In fact, I think she told me that she was the one who fired him,' Mahi said shaking her head.

'But how did she know that he was your friend?' Samrat asked.

'Well, if you must know, we were talking about our college days and I ended up showing her pictures of us. She recognized him and told me about him,' Mahi said rolling her eyes.

'Did you ask her where he went? Did you get his address, his contact number… anything at all?' Krish asked her agitatedly.

'No, I wanted to, but by then Sid was so furious with me for embarrassing him that I did not ask her anything further. In fact, he was right after all, we do have a reputation to maintain, I can't just go around messing up things for myself while trying to fix the life of someone who doesn't have a clue,' Mahi said looking at Akshii trying to make her understand. When it became quite clear to her that once again Dorky's mistakes would be pinned upon her, she got up saying, 'Now, if you'll excuse me please. I think I need to go to the powder room.'

All of them watched as she got up and swayed away from

them. Krish exclaimed in disbelief, 'I swear to god sometimes I have no idea how she does it. No wonder everybody thinks she is a bitch. She behaves like a diva even around friends.'

'C'mon Krish, you know that's not true. She loves all of us and she has always thought about us before herself,' Akshii said defending Mahi. Kabir snorted at the statement and Akshii gave him such a stern look that he started to look around just to avoid her.

Truth be told, she knew that Mahi did come across as a selfish person sometimes, but she also knew that once you got to know her, she was the most caring person in the world. She knew from first-hand experience that Mahi would go to any lengths for her friends, just like she had helped out Akshii on a number of occasions.

As Akshii looked at the faces of her friends, she couldn't help but reminisce. Even though there had been countless memories she cherished, the day she had met Mahi was the most memorable one for her. That day was special not because she and Mahi were best friends or long-lost sisters, but quite the opposite, because they were so completely different from each other. It was that day that she had realized that Mahi, as superficial as she seemed, would go to any lengths for her friends.

≈

10

The Pinch-Hitter

SHE REMEMBERED HER very first day in college, when her parents dropped her off, just before the orientation programme began. 'Ai-aiyoo! My daughter's very first day in college, such a blessed day. Kamakshii, we must plan a trip to Tirupati to thank god for showing us this day,' Kamakshii's mother said, folding her hands and reciting the name of every god she knew under her breath.

Akshii rolled her eyes and complained to her dad, 'Appa, mom's doing it again. Would you please ask her to stop? I'll get late for my orientation.'

'Oh Pudgy! Let your mom do her pooja, after all, this is a big day for all of us. Okay, tell me, did you talk to Ainvi?' asked Akshii's dad, trying to draw her attention away from her mom who was still thanking all the gods in the universe.

'I tried. But she didn't pick up or call back. How rude. She always does that. She knows how important this day is for me. But still, she didn't call. And please, Appa, do not take her side. You always do that,' she complained.

'Pudgy, she must be busy. You know how hard she had to study to get into that college, and it's her final year. I'm sure she will call you. She is elder than you, you must always remember that,' her dad said, rubbing her sister's success in her face for the millionth time.

'But last night you said that because I am an elder sister, I should be more benevolent, caring, and forgiving. You also said that being the younger sister means that you're almost expected to be the brat,' Akshii said grudgingly.

'Pudgy, c'mon, you know your little sister adores you and she was picking a fight just because she is going to miss you so much. That's why I said that,' her dad answered, his voice dropping to a whisper because he knew what would follow.

'Ugh, Appa! It's just not fair! I don't want to be the middle one! If it's not apologizing to one, it's forgiving the other one. Why do I have to do everything? Also, can you please stop calling me Pudgy! I put on a little weight ten gazillion years ago and my own father won't stop calling me that! Do you really want me to have an eating disorder?' Akshii ranted without pausing for breath while getting out of the car.

'Kamakshii, that's no way to talk to your Appa. And where is your bindi, you can't go in without that,' her mother said, fishing out a packet from her own purse and sticking one onto Akshii's forehead.

'Okay, now can I go in? Please, I am getting late,' Akshii said, defeated, giving her mom and dad a last cursory hug.

'Oh Pudgy, I am going to miss you so much. Call us, okay, anytime you want. I know you feel that we love your sisters more, but I love all of you the same,' her dad whispered in her ear as her mother wiped the corner of her eye with a dainty little handkerchief.

She gave them a huge smile and then turned around and ran all the way till she was in the conference hall, and frantically looked for a seat. She found an empty one, and she rushed and plopped into it.

'Ugh! Slow down. Where's the fire?' exclaimed the girl sitting next to her.

Akshii turned to apologize, and looked at the girl sitting next to her for the first time. 'Sorry,' Akshii muttered, and looked at her from head to toe and as if reminded by it, removed the bindi from her own forehead.

'Oh, it's okay, it's just that I didn't get enough sleep last night. You know, I went out with these really cute guys yesterday, friends of my friends, but it was so much fun! We went to Butter, they have really nice salad. Have you ever been there?' she babbled on.

'Um, no, I am new here,' Akshii said, trying to concentrate on the orientation.

'Hey, so am I,' the girl exclaimed. 'In fact, just reached yesterday.'

'But I thought you just partied yesterday,' Akshii asked confused.

'Yeah, so?' The girl asked, equally confused.

Akshii shrugged, deciding that the girl next to her had definitely wandered off a different planet. She secretly hoped that there would be a galaxy of distance between them.

As the orientation proceeded, Akshii fought to keep her attention focused on the dean, despite the constant buzzing in her ear. With each sentence came a new question from her neighbour's mouth, 'Are they serious? Nine o'clock curfew?' or 'How can we have an 8-hour class schedule, I will have dark circles under my eyes!' Once they were done with the orientation, they were asked to check with the administration to find out their allotted rooms and roommates.

Akshii walked from the academic block to the hostel, following the directions mentioned in the pamphlet. In her hand she held a bunch of keys for the room door and other fixtures.

She heard someone call out from behind. She turned around to see the girl who had sat next to her during orientation wobble along the gravel path in her five-inch heels. 'Hi. I am going to go set up my room,' Akshii said courteously as the girl caught up with her.

'Oh, me too! That is, if I get to my room without breaking my legs. I mean, who in their right minds doesn't have a road in campus, all this sand and gravel. I swear I will have to wear flats. Can you imagine...UGGH. Anyway, what's your room number? Maybe I can stop by after settling in, and then we can get something to eat,' she said, following Akshii down the gravel path.

At that moment, Akshii's phone rang shrilly, and for the first time, she wanted to thank all the gods in the universe too. Smiling a little, she said, 'Sorry, I need to take this, it's my sister. I guess we'll catch up sometime.'

Without waiting for the girl to respond, Akshii picked up the call and started talking. Even though she was really mad at her sister, she was so thankful for an opportunity to walk away from the girl, that she wholeheartedly forgave her. She told her sister all about her day, and about how she had met this girl who had instantly got on to her nerves. She was so engrossed in her conversation that she didn't even realize that she had reached her room and opened the door. She put down her bag on one of the single beds, lay down on it and continued to talk. Just as she was describing to her sister the comic sight of seeing her wobble in those humongous heels, a chirpy voice from outside the room said, 'Hey, is this your room, too?' Akshii's heart sank as she recognized the voice and hung up the call saying, 'Di, I will call you later. Bye.'

'What are you doing here?' Kamakshii asked, as the voice was followed by the girl laden with luggage.

'What do you think, silly? This is my room, I mean our room. I am Mahi, by the way, we never exchanged names. Isn't it weird, even after sitting next to each other since morning, we didn't introduce ourselves to each other. So, what's yours?' she asked excitedly, throwing her stuff everywhere.

'What's mine?' Akshii asked dazed.

'Name, silly! What's your name?' Mahi asked.

'Oh, Kamakshii,' she said, still reeling from the shock.

Mahi stumbled in with her immense bags and plopped on the opposite bed saying, 'Aaah! My feet are killing me. Sometimes I wonder if these heels were created by some man who hated girls and just wanted to see them suffer. You know what I mean, Akshii?'

'Akshii?' she asked puzzled.

'Oh it's just that your name is so big, I thought this one suits you better,' Mahi said, with the sweetest smile.

Akshii did not have the faintest of idea of how to respond, but by now, she knew it was better not to say anything at all, and just nodded along. Making an effort, she attempted to find something in common, 'Wow, you brought all this stuff up at once. You must have amazing upper body strength. Do you play tennis or volleyball or something?'

'Oh, this isn't all the stuff, I still have three big ones downstairs—I paid the guards to bring them. And I don't really play anything, but I do shop a lot, so maybe that's why. Hey, it's getting a little late, do you want to go get something to eat?' Mahi asked.

'Um, no actually... looks like you have a lot of unpacking to do. I also need to settle down, besides, we have classes tomorrow,' Akshii said, excusing herself.

'Oh my god! Are you always this "goody-two-shoes" or is today a special occasion?' Mahi pouted.

'Are you always this snippy, or is today a special occasion?' Akshii retorted.

Mahi looked at Akshii and said, 'Okay fine, truce! Look, both of us have to live together, and presently, both of us will have to eat. C'mon, it just might be fun for both of us. I'm sure by now you have realized that we are poles apart. Let's try to find an equator and make both of our lives easier.'

Akshii stared at Mahi for a moment, thinking it over, and then said, 'All right, what the hell!'

'Great, let's get ready,' Mahi said, messaging someone on her phone. Once she was done, she opened up her bags and started to rummage through. them By the time she was finished, their room looked like a war zone, filled with clothes and accessories thrown everywhere. While Mahi zipped around changing and accessorizing, Akshii grabbed a t-shirt amidst the chaos and started to change.

Once Mahi was ready, which felt like eons to Akshii, they both went downstairs, and to Akshii's surprise, there was a car waiting for them. Mahi quickly gave directions to the driver and sat back and relaxed. The car ride was heavy with silence, as neither had anything to say to the other. Just as Akshii started to have second thoughts, Mahi said, 'We are here. Come, let's go in.'

Mahi glided over to the reception and said, 'Hey, table for two.'

'Sorry, we are overbooked today. Would you mind waiting for forty-five minutes?' said the snooty reception girl, giving her an icy look.

'Oh sweetie, I don't wait for anyone. So, why don't you just check again?' Mahi answered, returning look for look.

'I did...twice. So, if you don't mind stepping away,' said the receptionist with a plastered smile.

'Actually Sana, Miss Mahi does have a table. The best one, in fact,' said the manager, swooping in from behind the receptionist.

'I don't understand. There's no booking in her name,' the receptionist responded confused.

'Yes, well, they have one under my name. So, why don't you take them inside and show them to the table, or actually, let me,' he said, quashing the conversation once and for all.

Once they were seated, Mahi thanked the manager and whispered something to him. Mahi turned to Akshii with a devious smile which made her put down her menu and finally ask, 'What! Why are you looking at me like that? Spit it out, Mahi. Actually, forget it. Can we please order, I am starving.'

'Sure. What do you want? Don't bother with the drinks; I hope you don't mind, I have already placed an order for those,' Mahi bubbled.

Akshii looked at her in disbelief, understanding the secret of her smile and said, 'I don't drink, Mahi. I never have and I don't intend to start now. So, could you please keep these crazy ideas to yourself?'

'Have you ever tried it? Well, don't knock it before you try it,' Mahi said, with mischief in her eyes as the waiter set the shots on the table.

'No Mahi, we can't, we are girls. It's not right or safe,' Akshii exclaimed.

'What? Are you kidding me? Did you just pull the gender card on me, darling?' Mahi sputtered on the shot she had just downed. 'Puh-lese, what has our being girls to do with drinking, or for that matter, with anything at all? And I learnt this way back: if we consider ourselves the weaker sex, then the world is more than ready to run us through with their MCP ideas. Akshii, men are in no hurry to give us the crown of the world. We have to fight our own battles, even if we're in our own pointy little shoes,' Mahi said bitterly.

'Wow! I didn't know you felt so strongly about this. But still, we live in India, and boys and girls are brought up differently. A boy can drink, go out at night, and do whatever he pleases... a girl on the other hand is always told to stay within certain limits. It's just how the world works,' Akshii tried to defend her stand.

Mahi chuckled and said, 'Kamakshii, these so called 'limits' are set by the same people who rape girls and then defend themselves by saying that the girl was dressed in a certain way, or that she was behaving promiscuously. They can say whatever they want, but all I know is that a two-year-old or a three-year-old child, or for that matter any girl, is in no way responsible for the actions of some perverted man. Besides, I thought you were a total tomboy. I didn't find even a single pair of decent heels in your stuff.'

'You went through my stuff! That's out of bounds, Mahi. And yes, I am a tomboy, but that doesn't mean I want to drink. I'm leaving,' Akshii said, looking flabbergasted. She got up and stormed towards the main door, without giving Mahi a backward glance.

Fuming and worrying about how to get back to college, Akshii tried to cross the over-crowded dance floor, when suddenly she froze. Silent tears started to roll down her cheeks, and she felt someone grab her hand and lead her towards a table. Shaking madly, she didn't even look up until Mahi sat down and asked her, 'Akshii, what's the matter? I was right behind you, and you started crying in the middle of the dance floor. Listen, if you don't want to drink it's okay, you don't have to cry. Wow, I never thought you were one of those girls.'

After a few moments, during which Akshii sobbed silently, and Mahi pestered her with questions, she finally said gulping down tears, 'Mahi, I don't know what happened to me, I feel so humiliated. It's not like me at all. I have been around boys all my life, I even played for my school's boys' volleyball team. But this has never, ever, happened to me. That guy, in that disgusting orange t-shirt, you will not believe what he did... he pinched my ass.'

Mahi laughed and said, 'Seriously, why didn't you slap him? And this has never happened to you before? Are you for real? Besides, it just proves my point. Okay, stop crying. C'mon Akshii! Ok what if I tell you we can teach him a lesson that he will never forget?'

'How? Should we go and kick him in his balls? Or should

we just beat the hell out of him? Or, I know, why don't you go and smash your high heel into his foot… he will never walk again,' Akshii said suddenly excited, shaking her head madly.

'Whoa! These babies are not doing anything of that sort… they are originals. But I do like the way you think. Stick with me, baby and someday you may outshine me. For now, calm down and just enjoy the show. I assure you this is one night you will never forget in your entire life,' Mahi said, getting up and walking towards the dance floor.

She sneaked up behind the guy in the orange t-shirt, who was busy dancing sleazily, and pinched his ass. The guy jumped as if he had been electrified, and stared at her as if she had come from a different planet. He hurriedly created some distance between her and himself. Mahi, however, unperturbed by the reaction, silently sneaked up behind the guy again, and pinched him a second time. The guy, who by now had clearly become unhinged, moved to the extreme opposite of the dance floor while keeping an eye on Mahi, who started to trail him slowly. After the whole charade went on for another ten minutes, by the end of which the guy was literally running in circles on the dance floor, Akshii was in splits of laughter. He quickly paid his bill and ran from the dance floor, but not before Mahi had sneaked up behind him one last time, and pinched him so hard that he yelled out 'Mummy!' Unfortunately for him, this happened at the exact moment the DJ changed tracks, and his voice echoed through the pub in that fraction of silence.

'Ta-Da!' Mahi exclaimed as she came back, and they laughed for another fifteen minutes. Once they were done, she smiled at Akshii and said, 'Listen, I am sorry, I shouldn't have pushed you. Let's get something packed and then go back. We have classes tomorrow morning, and you definitely don't look the sort who likes being late.'

'Actually, I think you were right. I shouldn't knock out things before I try them. What do you say... Will you order for me? I have no clue as to what's what?' Akshii said smiling back, knowing that this would be the first of a long list of firsts for her, and the start of a brand new friendship.

≈

11

Still Water

A S DAMODAR WALKED in, he noticed that there were many eyes shooting him curious glances. *'Probably trying to remember my name,'* he muttered to himself. *'Not that it's going to matter in a few hours. In fact, in a few hours, everyone will remember my name,'* he thought, itching to reach for the weapon in his pocket. But he told himself to be patient.

He walked slowly looking at the happy faces around him. Each time he heard laughter, he thought they were laughing at him; each time he crossed a table, he felt them whisper about him to each other. And just when he felt he was going to lose his mind, he caught a glimpse of her and a sense of calm spread over him.

As if in a trance, he started to walk towards her. Even today, he couldn't breathe at the sight of her. She still laughed the same way, talked and gestured exactly the same way, in fact, just by looking at her, no one would ever guess that ten years had passed.

Was he doing the right thing? For the last few weeks, he

had struggled with the question of morality. He needed a drink, but before that, he needed to find a place from where he could watch them while he built up his courage.

He knew that at some point he would have to go and talk to them to put his plan in motion, but right now, as he saw Mahi laughing, all he wanted was to crawl into some dark space and never come out. He sighed as he thought to himself, *'She looks perfect, too bad she has to die so soon.'*

He moved to the table at the opposite end of the room, from where he could watch them without hindrance. Once the waiter appeared, he ordered a rum and coke. The waiter looked at him and said, 'Sir, it's an open bar. Are you sure you don't want anything else?' Damodar gave him a look which threatened physical violence, and the waiter took the hint and left.

'Dorky! Damodar!' Kabir exclaimed, as he came out of the loo wiping his hands.

Dorky, who looked as if someone had just caught him red-handed, looked at him anxiously and said extending his hand, 'Hi.'

Kabir looked at the hand for a moment and then slapped it away saying, 'Oye, what's up, bro? Gimme a hug.'

'Huh, yeah sure,' Dorky got up, still looking as if someone had caught him making off with the cutlery.

'You know, I saw your name on the guest list on the notice board. And I thought to myself, why did they have to go through the trouble of writing your complete name: Damodar Kumar Yadav? Couldn't they just pick out the right alphabets and write "Dorky"? We figured it out in the first year of college, and these morons will take eons to reach there,' said Kabir, taunting him. 'Anyway, I am just babbling. When did you come? We were all waiting for you. And why are you sitting here? We're all sitting over there. Didn't you see us?' Kabir, trying to extricate himself from the awkward situation, pointed towards their table, where Krish was talking quite animatedly. By the stricken look on Akshii's face, Damodar judged that it was probably about a girl.

'I just reached. I didn't know whether you guys were here or not, so I decided to sit down here,' Dorky said, giving him a feeble grin.

'Well, now you know. C'mon man, let's go. Everybody is waiting for you,' Kabir said, putting a hand on Damodar's shoulder and walking towards the table. Dorky cursed his gods, and with every step, his pulse quickened until all he could hear was his own heart thumping as loud as a drum. He looked at Kabir nervously, wondering if he could hear the voices screaming in his own mind.

'Look who I found hiding in the shadows, guys,' Kabir announced.

'Oh, I wasn't exactly hiding,' Dorky said quickly in his defence. Realizing that he needed to calm down or else they would learn of his plan, he quickly smiled and vanquished any signs of anxiety from his voice.

Once they had all settled down, Dorky braced himself for the plethora of questions he could see lingering in their eyes. *'Well, they will have their answers soon, and I shall have mine,'* he thought to himself and immediately felt his pulse relax.

'So, how have you been Dorky?' Krish asked first.

'Here we go,' Dorky thought to himself. 'Fine, as always I guess. How are you guys?' he asked, returning the question.

'Good. Everything is good,' Krish said.

'Oh yeah, all of us are good. Infact, we were just talking

about how long it has been since we all were together,' Akshii said, smiling. But before she could say anything further, Krish gave her a wide-eyed stare, the sign to change the topic.

As if on cue, Shiksha swayed towards their table, waving at Krish. She leaned in to whisper in his ear in a sultry voice and breath laced heavily with alcohol, 'Hi, Krish.'

Krish got up to give her a hug, which pretty much ended with him balancing her, 'Hi Shiksha, you look good.'

'Oh, tell me something I don't know. Um, you look yummy too,' she said, checking him out from head to toe as if he was made of chocolate. Just as suddenly, noticing Kabir, she exclaimed, 'Kabir, dah-ling!'

'Hi, Shikhs…,' Kabir said, getting up quickly to catch her, as Krish literally threw her towards him. Mahi gave them such a look that the others could not supress their grins.

Shiksha greeted the group warmly, but gave Mahi an icy look and still leaning on Kabir said, 'So, I see you guys still keep the same company. Tch-tch. Guys, change is good you know.'

'Oh, is that why you have moved on to your third husband?' Mahi asked, mocking.

'Mahi, dah-ling… I didn't notice you. Well, anyway, Kabir, Krish, always a pleasure,' she said, landing a peck on their cheeks and slipping a card into Krish's pocket before walking away.

'I hate that bitch,' Mahi said, disgusted.

'Well, it looks like the feeling's mutual, dah-ling,' Samrat said, mimicking Shiksha.

'Looks like she hasn't gotten over the old rivalry,' Dorky said grinning.

'Well, good for her. By all means, let her hold a candle to it all her life. I am above all this childishness,' Mahi said snootily.

'Well, you did call her boyfriend "monkey-faced".' Akshii said, reminding her.

'Oh please, she said I was trying to lure him away. Him! As though I had nothing better to do all day but stare at his monkey face. I don't see what she was complaining about, she could've had him to her heart's content, nobody ever wanted him anyway,' Mahi said.

All of them burst into laughter and Akshii said in between snorts, 'C'mon, you have to admit that it was below the belt. God, you were so immature.'

'I was immature? Really? And what about you Miss Kamakshii, do you remember your fights? Of course you don't, let me remind you,' Mahi said narrowing her eyes, grinning as Akshii's expression turned to stone.

'Mahi, you shush,' Akshii said threateningly.

As they all laughed, with and at each other, Dorky started to remember his college days. While all they talked about were the sweet ones, all Dorky could remember was the day all his dreams had been shattered. The first step to the end of his life.

12

Glass-House Shatters

DORKY COULDN'T HELP but remember the fateful day all his dreams had crumbled right before his eyes in a span of a few moments. He had heard others say that college memories never fade, but only grow fonder as time passes. But whenever he thought about his college, all he remembered was that day—everything else was a blur.

Even now, as he sat at the same table and looked at his so called 'friends', he could not help but reminisce about the moment it all had started. He had heard survivors say that their life had changed in a second—a minute ago they had been living their lives without a care in the world, and a minute later it was all gone. He remembered how his morning had started with such promise, with absolutely no sign of the brooding storm that would hit him later.

As soon as he had opened his eyes that morning, he started to think about how that day was going to be the start of his new life. He smiled at the thought, positively giddy. Reluctant to get out of his bed, he snoozed his alarm clock and decided to do that one thing that he hadn't done in his entire college life...bunk a class.

He laid back and started to visualize his perfect evening. Every wish in his life would be fulfilled. A fully-paid scholarship to study in an Ivy League college, a degree to die for, lucrative job offer that would be a piece of cake after graduating and to top it all, his dream girl in his arms and the world at their feet.

He rolled over and took out Mahi's picture from under the mattress. He looked at it, marvelling at how perfect she was. *'Oh my god, I love her so much. And today, after my scholarship results are announced, well officially, I will tell her. I hope she accepts.'* His heart quickened at the thought. *'Of course she will, she loves me too, it's just that she is too afraid to say it out loud. Besides, if she doesn't love me, why does she rely on me for everything?'* he reassured himself.

Dorky kissed the picture and hid it in its usual place. As he stared at the ceiling thinking that since he had already decided to bunk the class, why not catch up on some lost winks, and closed his eyes. After a few minutes, he woke up and looked around the room, wondering why he had woken up so soon. His eyes wandered to the clock on the side table, and he sat up with a jerk as he saw the clock on the side table indicating that three hours had passed.

He jumped out of bed, cursing his stupid cell phone which had failed to sound the alarm and saw that the battery had died. *'Shit, I don't even have time to charge it now,'* he thought to himself and left it on the bed. He ran out of the room, locked it, and hobbled down the corridor putting his pants on. As he reached the bike stand, he fished out his keys.

Just as he was glaring at the stupid machine, willing it to

start, he heard someone behind him smirk, 'Hey Dorky! It's push start.'

He turned around to see Gaurav walking towards the mess door with his eyes half-closed. 'Umm… What does that mean?' he asked, confused.

Gaurav rolled his eyes and said, 'See that red button, push it.'

Dorky pressed the button and the bike sprang to life. He gave Gaurav a sheepish smile and reversed. As he was putting on the helmet, Gaurav looked at him sceptically and asked, 'Are you sure you can drive this, nerd? Not that I care about you, but that's a beautiful piece of machinery. How did you get Krish to lend you the bike?'

Dorky shook his head, grumbling, and drove forward cautiously, deciding not let his spirits get quashed for any reason today. Although he had driven Krish's bike a few times, it had always been while Krish was riding pillion. Deciding to focus on the task at hand he sped up and concentrated on the road.

Had it not been for the flowers and chocolates that he had to pick up for Mahi, he would have grovelled a bit more and asked Krish to drive him but this was kind of a big secret for him.

A smile crossed his face. He mentally listed all the things he needed for tonight, and started to calculate the amount of time he needed to finish all the errands and get back to college before the big announcement.

Once he reached the city market, he ran around in circles getting things done. The florist wrapped up the bouquet of roses grumbling under his breath—not only had he wasted half an hour because he insisted on hand-picking the flowers himself—now it looked as if he was gearing up to negotiate over a few rupees.

Dorky looked at his watch and pushing the money into the shopkeeper's hand, hurried up. He packed everything into his bag, handling the flowers gently. The ride back would take almost an hour, and he had to be careful that they did not get squished.

Mentally ticking off items from his list, he checked if he had everything and decided to leave. He wanted to make this evening perfect—many other guys had already tried it, but he knew Mahi better than them. He knew that she was not the kind of girl who could be won with just flowers; she needed the best of everything.

The 45-minute ride felt much shorter to him today as he reached the hostel parking lot. He parked the bike, ran up the stairs to his room and yanked open the door. As soon as he stepped in, he opened his bag, pulled out the flowers delicately and gently placed them in a half-filled glass. He sat down to admire them, imagining the reaction they would get from Mahi.

Just then, someone banged on his door bringing him back to earth. A voice yelled from the other side, 'Hey Dorky! Open up man.'

Irritated, he got up and opened the door and an even more irritated Gaurav shoved his phone in his hand saying, 'It's for you.'

Dorky gave him a confused look which peeved Gaurav even more. 'Look, I haven't got all day! Besides, I have already come up to check on you three times. Will you just talk?'

Dorky put the phone to his ear and said, 'Hello?'

He heard another voice screaming at him from the other side. 'Dorky, where the hell have you been? And why in the world is your phone switched off? Whatever, we will talk about that later. Listen, the dean has already asked to see you three times since morning. You need to come here right now,' Krish yelled.

'What? What does he want? I thought the announcement was not till later this afternoon. Did they move it up?' Dorky asked, with his heartbeat racing.

'Look, this is not the time to discuss this, you need to come immediately, just leave everything and come, Dorky,' Krish said, his voice full of urgency.

Dorky thrust the phone back into Gaurav's hands and ran downstairs. Gaurav's voice followed him, 'Yeah, don't bother thanking me.'

He ran all the way till the academic block which was easily a kilometre away.

Krish was waiting for him at the main gate. As Damodar tried to catch his breath, he said, 'You ran... why? You have my bike, why didn't you use that?'

Dorky wheezed and tried to answer. Just then, Akshii yanked Dorky by his hand saying, 'Krish, we need to get him upstairs, leave your interrogation for later.' She dragged him towards the dean's office and pushed him inside even before there was an answer to the knock.

Dorky gulped hard due to the lack of breath and the nervousness of being in the dean's office didn't help either. Taking a long breath he said, 'Sir, you wanted to see me.'

The dean gave him a look which clearly expressed his displeasure, and beckoning him to a chair said, 'Yes, in fact, I have been trying to see you since morning, Mr Damodar.'

'I am really sorry, Sir. I wasn't feeling well. I was sleeping. I am really sorry if you had any trouble because of me,' Dorky said, giving him a weak smile while he sat down.

The dean raised his eyebrow and said, 'Really, that's interesting, since your friends told me that it was your legal guardian who was hospitalized and you had gone to see him.'

Dorky looked as if someone had thrown him under the train as he stared at the dean and then at the door, speculating how much trouble would he be in exactly, if he ran out of the room screaming? 'Sir, actually, I think they got it a bit confused… what happened was that I was unwell, so my legal guardian called me saying that he was in the hospital waiting, and so I went, Sir.'

'And how, if I may ask, did he know that you were so unwell?' the dean asked, clearly enjoying himself. Dorky looked at him as if he had been asked to disprove one of Einstein's theories.

'Fine, let it be. Besides, we have more important things to discuss today,' the dean said, pulling out a file named Damodar Kumar Yadav. He flipped it open and gave it a cursory glance. 'So, I see that you have applied for the scholarship.' Dorky nodded with fervent raptness, shifting uncomfortably with excitement.

'Your grades seem to be perfect,' the dean smiled politely. 'I am glad to see that. In fact, with these grades, you will get a pick of your choice for colleges and even jobs.' Dorky smiled genuinely for the first time since he had entered that office and looked up to thank the dean, but his smile flattened when he saw the dean's grim expression.

'Sir, is there any problem?' Dorky asked.

'Well, look, there is no easy way to say this. But you must understand that this does not mean that you have no other options. In fact, it means that a whole new world of opportunities has opened up for you. It's just that Harvard wants someone with more than just educational qualifications; they want someone who is an all-rounder,' the dean said, looking sombre.

'All-rounder? What does that even mean?' Dorky asked, hysterical.

'They want someone who has participated in some extra-curricular activities, beyond just books. Someone like Samrat. See, he has participated in cultural events, played in some matches, and he is the president of the chess club,' the dean said, explaining.

'Samrat. You are giving it to Samrat. How can you do that? I have spent the last three years preparing for this scholarship, and now you are telling me that I don't have it,' Dorky said crazed.

'Damodar, calm down,' the dean said understandingly.

'No, I will not calm down! You wanna know why I don't have any extra-curricular activities in my file? That's because while the others were out doing those things, I was grinding my ass studying. All my life I have been preparing for this day. You can't do this. You can't give him my spot. I have better grades than him. Do you think I don't know why you are giving him the scholarship? It's only because he is more popular,' Dorky yelled while tears brimmed in his eyes.

'Damodar, behave yourself. We don't encourage our students to behave like hooligans under any circumstances. Besides, Samrat's grades are almost at par with yours, and he has other experiences,' the dean said, raising his voice.

Chastised, Dorky started pleadingly with him, 'Sir, my whole life depends on this. Please, don't do this to me. Please, Sir. Just send my name. I promise, you won't regret it.'

'I am sorry Damodar, we have never had a rejection from Harvard till date, and if we send in your name, even after they have specified their criteria, I'm afraid the answer will be in the negative. We can't take the risk,' the dean said with a sigh.

'But, Sir...,' Dorky started to say, but was interrupted by the dean.

'Look Damodar, I can give you recommendations and help you with your applications personally, but I'm afraid I can't give you this scholarship,' the dean said, putting an end to the conversation, and started to sift through some other papers on his desk.

Dorky sat there looking at the 'now pretending to be busy' dean and wondered whether his legs would be able to support his weight if he rose from his chair. Finally, he got up with the support of the table, and walked out of the door.

Krish, Akshii, Kabir and Samrat were sitting outside. When they saw him, they got up. 'Dorky, what's wrong? What did he say? Is everything okay?' Kabir asked concerned.

'Why isn't he saying something?' Akshii asked scared.

Samrat shook him by the shoulders and asked, 'Dorky, what happened?'

'You got the scholarship, Samrat,' Dorky said quietly.

'What?' Samrat asked surprised. Just like everyone else, he had expected Dorky to win the scholarship. All of them looked quizzically at each other, and for once, they did not know how to react.

Samrat, the first to recover, said putting a hand on Dorky's shoulder, 'I am so sorry, Dorky. Trust me, I never thought they would give it to me. But you know, this is not the end of the world. I am sure you can apply at other places.'

Dorky slapped away the hand and yelled, 'I don't want anything else; this is my scholarship. You stole it from me. You are the reason behind it, so don't even pretend that you are sorry. Get away from me! I don't need any one of you!' He started backing away from them, while all of them looked aghast.

Dorky knew he was walking, but did not know where he was going. His feet were carrying him in a random direction. He had heard somewhere that when your body is in shock it can't feel any pain. Perhaps that was what was happening to him—he couldn't feel or think.

'Dorky!' He heard someone shout his name. He turned around to see Mahi hurrying towards him. The gravity of the situation hit him, and Mahi ran ahead to support him, as he had crumpled to his knees. 'Dorky, I am so sorry. Akshii just called and explained everything. Oh sweetie, I am so sorry. I know this must be very hard, but don't worry I am sure you will get through this.'

'Everything is lost. I have nothing to give you anymore,' Dorky said, hugging her. 'All our dreams are lost. It's all Samrat's fault. This is not how I had planned this, but Mahi, I promise I will give you everything. I just need some time.'

'What?' Mahi asked confused. 'Dorky...what in the world are you talking about?'

'I wanted to wait till the scholarship announcement to tell you that I love you and that I will give you everything that you have ever dreamt of. Don't worry, I will still be able to give you everything, but it will take me some time. But that's okay, if you are by my side I will do everything, and we will build our dream life together. Trust me,' Dorky said, holding her hand.

'What? No, Dorky, please stop. I have never thought of you like that. We are good friends. I mean, you know I am seeing Sidharth. Please, stop it,' Mahi said with a confused expression.

'No, that's not true. You are seeing Sidharth only because he is rich. You don't love him, you love me. That's why you always ask for me, whenever you need something, and I have always been there for you. I promise I will always be there for you,' Dorky said, confused by her reaction.

'Please, Dorky. Stop it. You are scaring me,' Mahi said, inching away.

'Mahi, you are my life. I will die without you. I will go insane! Please don't leave me, I have nothing left in my life. You are my only ray of hope. Please, Mahi. I will always keep you happy, just give me a chance,' Dorky pleaded, kissing her hand.

Mahi pulled away and said, 'I am so sorry Dorky, but you have always been just a very sweet friend. I don't love you in that way. Please get up.'

Dorky got up wiping his tears and gave Mahi one last pained look. He turned around and walked away while Mahi kept calling his name over and over again. A part of him died that day and he had no idea how to survive. But he knew one thing for certain—he needed to do it alone.

≈

13

Ripple Effect

'SO TELL US, what have you been up to all this time? I mean, you just vanished into thin air after the finals, Dorky. Are you okay? You seem a little pale, have you been keeping well? You look quite thin too, have you been eating properly?' Akshii blitzed him with questions which seemed endless.

'Akshii, let him breathe for a while. He'll be able to say something only if you give him a second in between,' Kabir interjected.

'Sorry! It's just that I want to know everything about him. God! It's been ages since we met and talked. We really missed you,' Akshii said.

Dorky smiled at her and he knew that the concern in her eyes was as genuine as the gun in his pocket. Out of the whole group, Akshii had been the most sympathetic; he would be sad to see her go. He took a deep breath and said, 'I know I haven't been around lately, but I am here now.'

'Well, would you mind if I asked you something? I have a lot of questions—we all do,' Krish asked hopefully.

'I guess,' Dorky said, shifting uncomfortably in his chair. 'What do you want to know?'

'Well, for starters, where the hell have you been all these years, man? We couldn't find you. Did you join RAW and become a spy or something? I mean, we all tried to look for you,' Kabir asked, leaning in.

'Unfortunately, nothing that exciting happened. I was busy with...life. Sorry, if I disappointed you guys. I am sure you were expecting something more, but I guess I am the same old person—dull and boring. My life is not as exciting as the lives you guys have,' Dorky smirked bitterly.

'Oh please, you talk as if we are some kind of adrenaline junkies, brother. I must admit, as much as I wish your words to be true, we are as mundane as you,' Samrat said politely, shaking his head.

'Speak for yourself, Dholki,' Mahi grinned, preening with fake arrogance.

Samrat folded his hands, grimaced and said, 'All hail Princess Mahi. We are so thankful that you could grace us with your highly valuable time. Will you kindly stoop to talk to us mortal souls, please? Or should we get you some offerings?'

'C'mon, for you guys, I am willing to slum it a bit,' Mahi grinned. Everybody broke out in laughter. She looked at Dorky and said, 'I am really happy to see you here. Truth be told, this night wouldn't have been complete without you. I might not say it often, but I have missed each and every person at this table a great deal.'

'Hear, hear!' Krish toasted. 'I am totally with you Mahi. So many things have changed in our lives now and yet, this feels just the same—familiar. I mean... this is just so... I mean...

um... you know.'

'Yeah, I know what you mean. It's like a void in our lives has been filled. Dorky, we really missed you man,' Kabir spoke, and Akshii wiped a tear from the corner of her eye.

'Akshii, are you crying?' Krish mocked. 'Oh hey, we need to get a bucket to collect her tears! Dorky, I guess you're getting a souvenir for this night.'

'Hey, you have two kids and try to stay impassive. And I am not crying, by the way! Jeez, you show a little sentiment and suddenly you're the talk of the town.'

Dorky gulped and smiled uncertainly, 'You have kids, Akshii?'

'Yeah, two boys, one's four and the other's thirty. They drive me mad but they are my whole world,' Akshii smiled.

'Oh, c'mon, your husband is not that bad. He is quite mature and responsible and he loves you so much. You just crib a lot,' Mahi said, pointing out her friend's fake complaints.

'Really, would you believe what my super-responsible husband did the last time he went outside the country? He lost his passport, just lost it, in a foreign land. Last week, he went to a meeting in a cab and left his cell phone there. Before that, we went out for dinner and he paid and left his card there... we actually had to go back the next day to collect it. Do you want me to go on?' Akshii laughed as she spoke in-between gulps from her drink.

'Oh, please. Count your lucky stars that that's your only problem. That man would give his life just to see you smile. He dotes on you, Akshii,' Mahi spoke while her gaze drifted far away.

Akshii blushed and said, 'Yeah, I am really lucky that way. And I know that I crib sometimes, and he drives me nuts sometimes, well actually more than sometimes, but I would give anything to spend my time with him.'

As Dorky listened to them talk, he felt an immense pain in his chest, as if someone had gripped his heart and started to squeeze it. He no longer felt that immense rage against his friends, especially when they looked genuinely happy to see him.

He got up suddenly trying to calm his inner turmoil, and said, 'I'm going to go get myself a drink.'

'Oh, you really don't have to, I can order it for you. Just let me know your choice of drink,' Krish interjected.

'Um, that's okay, I could do with a walk, and I should meet some other friends too,' Dorky said, shrugging and struggling to get away.

'You have other friends?' Krish said in mock anger and all of them laughed.

As he walked through the crowd of friendly faces, it struck Damodar how full of life the whole room seemed. With each step, the burden on his heart started to weigh him down even more. He couldn't breathe—all he wanted was to find some secluded place. He hastened towards the exit as inconspicuously as possible, trying not to black out. Once he reached the ground outside, he squatted down and breathed heavily.

His stomach churned as he thought about what he intended to do. He shook his head in disbelief and pulled out the gun to throw it away along with his plans. He knew that things hadn't worked out as he had expected them to, and the thought of killing his friends was making him sick.

'They are my friends, they love me. They care for me, why else would they be so concerned about me. It's not like they know what I've been going through. They care because I haven't met them in

so long. They even tried to look for me.' Dorky tried to explain it to himself, as if to a third person. He looked at the gun in his hand, which was getting heavier with every passing second. Just as he was about to throw it away, he heard laughter coming out of the hall. Alarmed, he quickly stashed the gun in his pocket and went back inside. He'd get rid of it as soon as possible. Once inside, his heart swelled at the thought of talking to his old friends. He quickly grabbed a drink and went back to the table.

'Let's get this party started. I have so many things to talk about, and so many things I need to say. But first, I want to know all about you guys. Akshii, I heard you have some pictures, or were you just kidding?' Dorky said with affection in his eyes.

As he sat down with a smile on his face, Mahi said, 'Oh good, you're back. I'm really glad to see you in such good spirits, considering what's going on in your life.'

'What do you mean?' Dorky asked.

'Oh... I heard that you had recently lost your job and were having a hard time finding a new one,' Mahi said, looking around for a way out.

'How did you know this, Mahi?' Dorky asked angrily.

'C'mon Dorky, just let it go man, it really doesn't matter. All that matters is that you stay strong through this,' said Kabir, trying to calm him down.

'You know about it too? Do you all know about it?' Dorky asked, aggression rising in his voice, shoving Kabir's hand away from him. 'Is that why you guys are being nice to me? You pity me?'

'Dorky, man, nobody pities you. We just wanna help,' Samrat added. 'We're just concerned, that's all.'

Dorky got up suddenly and edged away from them as if stabbed.

'Damodar, don't be like this. I know we should have said something before, but we were all so happy to see you here,' Akshii said, following him.

'You want to help me, fine. Let's go to our classroom,' Dorky said suddenly, oddly peaceful.

'What?' said Mahi, looking around, clearly confused. She saw her expression mirrored on her friends' faces as well.

'Yeah, I just need a fresh perspective towards life, and what better place to find it than our classroom where we dreamt of everything we wanted to be,' Dorky explained and smiled. 'C'mon guys. Wouldn't it be fun to see it again, revisit all those beautiful memories?'

'I don't know man, wouldn't it be closed?' Krish said.

'C'mon, all your life you've been breaking rules and now you suddenly care about them. Guys, what happened to you, you are the Fiasco Five! It will be fun! C'mon!' Dorky said.

'Yeah, let's go. It'll be fun. Besides, it's not just about a classroom, it's about us,' Samrat was the first to agree.

'I'm game too,' Mahi chirped.

'Fine, count me in too,' Akshii smiled at Dorky.

'C'mon guys, I'm not taking no for an answer. Let's do this one last thing together,' Dorky said.

'One last thing?' Kabir interjected and all of them turned to look at Dorky.

'I mean, for tonight, one last thing we do tonight. Guys, c'mon, don't make a mountain out of molehill,' Dorky said, covering up quickly.

'Okay, let's go,' Krish said, walking towards Dorky. 'Kabir, it's five against one. You don't have a choice now.'

'Fine, let's go. Anyway, you'd get scared of the dark if you went alone,' Kabir smiled as they all walked with their old friend to their classroom of ten years ago.

14

Classroom 1B

'IT'S LOCKED,' KRISH groaned as they reached the classroom. 'What now?'

'Can we break the lock?' Samrat asked, looking around to see if there was a guard present.

'Why do all boys think only about breaking stuff? Such a stereotype,' Mahi snorted.

'Mahi. We are not exactly peeing around the lock, are we? What other options do we have?' Krish said sarcastically.

'Yeah, apparently Krish knows a lot about peeing,' Kabir said, taking a jab at Krish, who glowered at him.

'Ew! And we could try opening it,' Mahi said, making a disgusted face.

'Oh! We could just open it! Did you hear that, Samrat? Hm, I wonder why we didn't think of that before... Well, maybe, because we don't have a key!' Krish shouted.

'Oh, you two. Thirty years old and you still fight like children. My son is more mature than both of you put together. I don't want to hear anything else,' Akshii said, raising her hand as they both opened their mouths to argue some more. 'Now, Mahi, can you still pick the lock?' she asked, turning towards her.

'Yeah, I can. But I'll need some space,' Mahi said, kneeling and pulling out a pin from her hair.

'You can pick a lock? Are you serious? Since when?' Dorky asked amazed.

'Ever since college, I guess. When you keep losing your keys as much as we did, an alternative is needed. And we couldn't exactly break locks, so we found another way,' Mahi said, working on the lock.

'Well, I thought you just fluttered those beautiful eyelashes at the guards and smiled or maybe flashed them,' Krish taunted.

'Krish!' both Mahi and Akshii said together, glaring at him.

'Jeez, sor-rry!' Krish said, putting up his hands as a sign of surrender. Akshii shook her head in disbelief.

Just then there was a small clink and Mahi said a second later, 'It's open... Can you help me up?' She extended a hand towards Kabir, who turned away.

'Here, let me help you,' Krish said, taking her hand. Mahi smiled sadly at him as she got up.

Samrat opened the door, walked in and took a deep breath. The others looked for the light switches.

Fumbling in the dark, Kabir said, 'Hey guys, I found it,' and switched on a tube light. They looked around their old classroom, which apart from some technological upgrades, had remained almost the same. Mesmerized, they gathered near the teacher's podium, and beamed at each other. Suddenly, struck by the same idea, they ran towards their old seats in unison, laughing.

Dorky alone remained standing. He smiled at his friends

and walked towards the door. As he latched it, he took a deep breath to focus.

He turned as Kabir asked, 'What are you doing, Dorky?'

'Oh nothing, I just shut the door so that we won't be disturbed,' Dorky said, smiling mysteriously.

'Hey, you guys remember when we used to give proxy for each other? Remember Dorky? I mean, the amount of proxy you and Dholki put for us was probably more than the number of classes we actually attended. I swear, you were a lifesaver,' Krish exclaimed.

'Interesting choice of words,' Dorky said under his breath, smirking. Kabir looked at his face and frowned. For some reason, he felt quite edgy and his friend wasn't exactly making it easy for him.

'Remember, we almost got caught one day by Prof. Pritam for giving proxy for you and Mahi,' Samrat exclaimed.

'Really... what happened?' Akshii asked surprised.

'Well, it wasn't a big deal, Dorky and I were asleep at the back, it was quite close to mid-terms and we had pulled an all-nighter. We didn't notice that there wasn't even one girl in the class that day. When your names came up, we automatically said "present", but we didn't notice the prof standing right beside us. Fortunately, the dean came in and shoved him away for some work,' Samrat said sniggering.

Dorky gave a pained smile that prompted Kabir to ask, 'Dorky, are you okay? You don't look too well. Maybe we should just go back.'

'No, no. I am fine,' Dorky said, smiling nervously. He immediately jumped onto the reminiscing bandwagon, 'Remember Hameer, he used to sit right in front. And remember how he used to sleep in class... Man, he was a legend. Once, when a teacher asked him if he was sleeping, he denied it. When the prof asked him about the topic they had been analyzing, he recited the whole discussion. How was he able to do that? How did he know what was going on in the class while sleeping? Maybe if I had that knack, I would not be here. I could never guess his secret then, and I don't think I'll ever get the chance to find out now.'

'Dorky, there's no secret. He was prompted by his friends. The profs just never caught them. Besides, he is right there in the ballroom, you can go and ask him. He will tell you, and even if he doesn't, all the other guys in their "gang" will tell you,' Samrat smirked and looked at Kabir, who for some reason had a deep frown on his face.

Dorky stood immersed in thought. 'You know, this place changed my life. I met you guys here, I built my dreams here, and then they were shattered right here.'

All the smiles vanished. 'That seat was where I sat. I thought that if I sat there hard enough, it would turn into a throne. My throne. I thought it would grant me all my wishes and bring the whole world to my feet. But I was so wrong.' He spoke as if he was trying to find the words to express something, but was unable to do so.

'Dorky, listen man, you look a little pale. Let's just go back and grab a drink. It will make you feel better,' Krish said, getting up and walking towards him. He put an arm around his friend and started to walk towards the door.

Just as they reached the door, Dorky jerked Krish's hand away saying, 'You know what, let's stay. I have a lot of things to talk about with you guys.'

'Sure, let's talk. But wouldn't it be more comfortable if we had some drinks and food?' Akshii said, trying to convince him.

'Well, I have had to go to bed with an empty stomach now and then, so hunger never bothers me. I get it if it bothers you, but humour me. Let's stay here for a while, and then we can all leave. I won't bother you anymore,' Dorky said in a mysterious voice.

They looked at each other uncomfortably and decided to stay, trying not to be rude. Kabir interjected, 'You know what Dorky, I think it will do you good too. Let's go back to the party. Once you see everyone, you will have fun too. Then we can sit back and have a long chat, just like you wanted. Sounds good?'

'Let's just stay here for a while, and then we can go back,' Dorky said, insisting.

Kabir put his foot down as well, 'No, you know what, I think we should leave now.'

The others looked at the duo as if they were watching a very uncomfortable tennis match.

Dorky sighed, shook his head and said, 'Yeah, I don't think I want to go back so I guess neither are you guys. See, the problem is that for once I don't really give a crap about what you want.'

'Come on Dork, cut it out,' Mahi said crossly.

'Oh yeah Ice Princess, make me!' Dorky said and gave them a crazed look.

≈

15

The Shot Heard Around the Room

'WHAT THE HELL are you doing, Dorky? Let's go! Now! This stopped being funny ten minutes back,' Krish said angrily.

'Pretty Boy! I'm afraid none of you will be leaving this room anytime soon. After all, we do have a lot to discuss,' Dorky smirked, pushing Krish back.

'You keep this up and I know one thing for sure—you are going to leave this room with a black eye,' Kabir roared.

'Okay! Guys, calm down. Dorky, this is not funny and you're creeping everybody out,' Akshii interrupted, trying to get the situation under control. Nothing had happened to worry her yet, but her gut was telling her to run in the opposite direction.

'Tell me Akshii, does your pathological need to be in control emerge out of your desire to be noticed? I mean, your parents don't love you as much they love your sisters, and even in this little group, Mahi has always been the apple of everybody's eye,' Dorky taunted.

'Okay, that's enough. You have gone too far! What is wrong

with you, Dorky? Apologize now!' Samrat intervened, placing himself between Kabir and Dorky.

'Oh, I think I must, now that the pauper has asked me to so nicely. Tell me Dholki, when did you become the king of the world? Was it when you took away my scholarship, or when you got that job with the eight-figure salary, or was it when you married Karuna?' Dorky said sarcastically.

'Oh my god, why in the world are you acting this way, Dork? And why in the world are we listening to you? Guys, let's get out of here,' Mahi said, turning towards the door.

Dorky blocked her before she could reach the door and whipped out the gun from his pocket. Mahi jumped back as if stung and stuttered, 'Dorky, is...that a gun?'

Everybody froze while Mahi stumbled back, her gaze fixed on the gun.

Krish, the first to recover, gulped and said smiling weakly, 'Dorky, c'mon man. You won man, all of us are officially punked. Good one, man.'

'You think this is a joke? Yeah, because everything is a joke to you, Krish Kapoor. Well, this is not a joke, this is my life, a constant nightmare. Congrats, now you get to be a part of this,' Dorky yelled, pointing the gun at all of them.

Samrat gulped and spoke soothingly while moving towards him, 'Damodar, what is wrong? Te...tell us, tell me!'

'Oh, now you want to know. Now that we have arrived at this stage, you want to have a tête-à-tête. Well, it's too little and it's too late,' Dorky yelled, shaking.

Kabir broke loose of the others and yelled while Mahi tried to hold onto him in vain, 'Listen you, son of a bitch. Let us go, right now, or I will rip you apart limb by limb with my bare hands! You think waving a gun in our faces is going to scare us? Well, I am not afraid and I will not be bullied by a loser.'

'You were always a pain, and you always had to meddle in everyone else's affairs. Had it not been for you, Krish would've gotten his ass kicked a thousand times in those years. Tell me, did he pay you to be his bodyguard, or were you just dumb enough to do it for free, Kabir?' Dorky smirked, knowing that even if Kabir wasn't scared, the others were, and they would never let anything happen to each other.

'Dorky, please yaar, why are you doing this? We have all been friends for so many years, what's wrong now?' Mahi asked with tears in her eyes.

'Me? A friend? Your friend? I was never your friend, I was just some groupie to you guys. "Dorky, do my homework. Dorky, I am hungry, get me something to eat. Dorky, I want to go to the market, get me an auto." Is that what you call friendship, because from where I'm standing, it looks like exploitation. All I ever wanted was to be a part of your precious group. That was my fault and I am paying for it. Heck, I have been paying for it since college. Now it's time all of you pay up as well,' Dorky said bitterly.

'We were nothing if not good friends to you! How many times did we save his ass from getting beaten up? Countless times Samrat helped him with his assignments, even when he was unwell we stayed by his bedside for a week. And you, Krish, god only knows how many times he has partied on your account. Did we ever keep a track of that? Did you?' Kabir roared.

'Well, you can consider it as payment for all the hoops I have had to jump through for you guys. Consider us even,' Dorky said, shaking with anger.

'Then why are we here, Damodar? If we are even, what more do you want from us? What in the god's name have we done?' Akshii asked, stepping forward, trying to make sense of the madness playing out in front of her eyes.

'All of you are here to answer for my life. My life, which you guys have ruined beyond belief. It's endless, the more I try to collect the pieces, the more they get scattered. Well I am done. Do you hear me, I am done!' Dorky snapped.

'Your life? What do you mean?' Mahi asked confused.

'Well, thanks to you guys, my life has been a string of failures. In the last ten years I have been fired from five different jobs. The last date I had was three years ago. There were days when even getting out of bed was difficult. I kept blaming myself and then one day it dawned on me: It's because of you guys that my life is in tatters,' Dorky yelled.

'So, we will help you pick up the pieces. Okay, I am sorry that we weren't there when all this was happening; we should have tried harder to find you. We all tried, but there were things happening in our own lives, and you just vanished after college. Dorky, we tried to contact you. And trust me, I will help you, we all will help you, get your life together. It's all going to be fine,' Samrat tried to reason with him.

'You think I need your help? Why? Because you guys are so special and you have magic wands? I don't need your pity!' Dorky yelled, waving the gun.

Mahi broke down and started to sob hysterically. Kabir immediately ran to her side and took her in his arms saying, 'Hey, hey, it's going to be alright. I promise nothing is going to happen to you. I would never let anyone hurt you.'

'Aw! If it isn't the Ice Princess and her court jester—or is it her lap poodle?' Dorky taunted.

Kabir got up shaking with rage, and in a flash before anyone could react, he thundered towards Dorky. Everyone screamed and lunged forward to catch hold of Kabir as both of them fought for the control of the weapon, but even before Samrat and Krish could intervene, a shot rang out and everyone froze...

16

The Only Way Out

EVERYBODY SHOOK FROM head to toe as they waited, holding their breath. Although it had been only seconds since the shot was heard, to them it felt as if eons had passed. Slowly, and as if in slow motion, Kabir stumbled back. Mahi shrieked as Kabir slumped and fell on the floor, hitting his head with a thud.

All of them ran towards him. Mahi, who was sobbing irrepressibly, crawled and sat beside him holding his head in an embrace. Krish turned and ran towards Dorky yelling, but Samrat caught him and forced him back. This, however, did not stop Krish from yelling through the tears running down his face. 'You shot him, you bastard! You shot him! He has always protected you, always stood up for you, and you shot him,' Krish yelled while Samrat tried to hold him back. 'Leave me, Dholki. He shot our friend. I will kill him.'

Dorky, who had pinned himself to the wall like wall paper, was staring at Kabir with a horror-struck expression. 'It's all his fault. He came at me. What was I supposed to do? I told him to back away, he didn't listen. I told all of you to stop. He didn't listen to me. Now, see,' Dorky rambled, with tears in his eyes and the gun shaking in his hand.

The gun was pointed at Krish, who was still struggling to get free and was shouting, 'Leave me, I am gonna kill him. Just let me go.'

Akshii came forward and stood in front of Krish. She took his face in her hands and said, wiping away his tears, 'Krish. Calm down please. Look, Kabir is hurt. We need to do something. This is not helping. Please calm down.'

Krish looked at Akshii and rushed back to Kabir. He started to shake him vigorously.

Mahi looked at them and started pleading, 'Krish! Please, please do something. What is wrong with him? Why isn't he waking up?' Krish looked at his hands; they were completely soaked in blood, which was now starting to pool around Kabir.

As Samrat bent forward to check on Kabir, Dorky screamed, 'Get away from him! All of you! Get away now.'

Samrat ignored him and crouched beside Kabir. He checked him limb by limb trying to figure out where the blood was coming from. He tried to roll him over but needed Krish to help him. He looked up when Krish didn't respond, and saw that he was still staring at his hands. 'Krish. I need your help. Krish!'

Akshii leapt forward and asked him, 'What do you need? Samrat, I am here, tell me.'

'I just need to figure out where this blood is coming from. Can you please help me roll him over? I have checked the front,' Samrat said.

As she bent over, Akshii tried but could not remember what she had done that morning. She started sobbing as they checked Kabir who was still unconscious. Samrat whispered,

'Akshii, listen to me and do not react. I know you are scared.' Akshii broke into silent tears while he found the wound and started to check it. 'Listen, please. Please listen to me... Akshii!' Samrat raised his voice trying to make her listen.

Akshii looked at him, tears still flowing, but something in Samrat's eyes made her regain control of herself. Samrat checked the wound and said, 'We have to do something, otherwise, none of us will get out of here.'

Akshii nodded and asked, 'What do you have in mind?'

'We'll have to stall him somehow, till someone starts to miss us,' Samrat whispered.

'Samrat, it's a reunion! Nobody is going to miss us. We need to make him see the error of his ways. Look, right now he thinks that his life is a mess because of us. If we could just reason with him...,' Akshii said.

'Akshii, this isn't our friend. He is a crazy person who has just shot a friend of ours. No, we need to call for help or call the police,' Samrat said with anger in his voice.

'Is he okay?' Dorky asked in a timid voice at that exact moment, trying to peer through the huddle.

'What do you think, Damodar? You shot him. No, he is not okay. He is losing blood and we need to get him some medical help. We need to call an ambulance,' Samrat spoke, wary of the crazed look on his former friend's face. 'Dorky, please. I beg you. If you have ever thought of us as friends, please let us take him to a hospital.'

'Is he dying?' Dorky asked Samrat point blank. 'Answer me, god dammit! Is he dying?' he asked again with such fierceness that the rest shivered.

'No, he is okay... for now! But if he keeps losing blood

then he won't make it,' he said, praying that Dorky would not catch the lie.

Samrat, who had already bound the wound, knew that Kabir was not critically injured. The bullet, fortunately, had only grazed his left shoulder and the bleeding would stop in some time. But he also knew that if Kabir regained consciousness, it would be impossible to control him. And if he got shot a second time, he may not be so lucky. Heck, all of them may get unlucky.

He knew that he had to act, and he had to act now. He had to stall Dorky till they could come up with an idea to get them out of this insane situation.

'Nobody is going anywhere, okay? This is no time to panic, this is exactly what I wanted. I can't back out of it now,' Dorky said, waving his gun. Although he was yelling, he seemed to be talking to himself more than anyone else.

'Dorky! Please tell me what we can do to help you? I mean, what do you want? Money? Because we can come up with that!' Samrat exclaimed.

'You think money can solve all your problems, don't you, Samrat? That's all you care about—money. Well, I don't care about your stupid money. Don't you get it? You are here to answer to me. Your money isn't going to help you now. I want you to pay for your sins, all of you. You will have to answer to me for ruining my life,' Dorky yelled, pointing his gun at Samrat.

'Will you please cut out this crap?' Mahi yelled so suddenly that Akshii almost jumped. Samrat looked at her and wanted to mouth out the word 'stop', but couldn't, because he didn't want to make any sudden movements. Dorky turned away from him and walked towards Mahi.

Samrat tried to block him, saying, 'Dorky, calm down please. She doesn't know what she is talking about. Please relax. You are right, we are sorry.'

'No we are not.' Mahi said indignantly. 'And what do you mean that we have to pay for our sins? What sins, Dorky? We were friends. If you didn't like something you could've always come up and said so. For god's sake, all of us were so immature,' Mahi yelled.

'Shut up,' Dorky said, clenching his teeth.

'No, I won't. You wanted answers right, well I want them too,' Mahi yelled fearlessly.

Dorky ran to her and put the gun to her forehead and yelled, 'I said shut up!'

Krish, who had been watching the whole scene like a statue, awoke from his trance and started yelling and pleading, 'Dorky, this is not...'

'No! Nobody interferes! Go on! Do it, get your revenge, Dorky! I hope you have better luck than I had in killing me,' Mahi yelled and closed her eyes. She had heard somewhere that when people faced death, their whole life flashed in front of their eyes. But for some weird reason all that flashed before her was the time she had spent with the people in this room.

As a tear rolled down her cheek, she realized that today she had been truly happy. In fact, she was happy after a long, long time, and she was fine bidding adieu to this world. She was at complete peace.

≈

17

Melting Ice

DORKY SWAYED BACK, as if jolted, and looked at her as if he could no longer recognize her. Mahi, unhinged by the sudden silence in the room, opened her eyes and was greeted by the grief-stricken faces of her friends.

'What?' Akshii said, unable to believe what she had heard.

Mahi shook with anger as she tried to speak. She knew that the glass facade she had carved for herself was breaking away, but for once, she did not care. She looked at Kabir's unconscious face and fresh anger flashed through her.

'What do you think Dorky, only you have problems in life? That your life turned out to be a nightmare, and all of us are living our dreams? Well, my 'dream' is also my cage—I can't even call it a nightmare because at some point a nightmare ends,' she said bitterly.

Mahi felt tears roll down her cheeks, but she knew that today all her inhibitions had been shattered. She could not breathe and started to speak again. She could hear the anguish in her voice but could not stop herself.

'You think that my life is like a fairy tale... all of you!' Mahi shouted. 'You think I don't know what people say about me? "Look at Mahi, isn't she so lucky, she has everything, she is wearing an Elise original, I would die to live her life," or "how does a girl like her get to live a life like that, she is so selfish, a first-class bitch, she is just so lucky." I guess everybody feels that way.'

'Nobody knows the truth about how I feel. Nobody cares, do they? Dorky, you say your life is a failure and you want to kill us for your own failures. Have you ever tried to kill yourself? Well, guess what, I have—not once, not twice, but thrice in the past ten years. Do you know what it feels like to hit rock bottom? To reach a point in life when you know for a fact that your life is inconsequential to everyone?' Mahi asked him.

'My friends loathe me, and I have no one to talk to. My life has no meaning—just an endless string of keeping up appearances. I am like a doll for everybody, "Mahi smile for the pictures, Mahi smile for my associates, Mahi do not sulk..." Failure. Do you even know what that feels like? Have you ever slept in the same bed where you know your husband has laid with an endless number of girls? Or do you know what it is like to pack his bags when you know that he is going to be with another woman? Well, I have, and I can't do anything about it because I can't go anywhere. To be trapped. That's failure,' Mahi broke down and sobbed irrepressibly.

'Mahi, sweetheart, why have you never said anything to me? You know I would have been there to help you. All of us would have,' Akshii spoke holding Mahi's hand. She felt guilty that her friend had been going through her life in such pain and she had no idea. She blamed herself—she knew that she should have kept in touch. The thought that the friend who had always fought with everyone was losing the fight of her life made her shiver.

The Mahi she knew was a survivor, but the woman sitting in front of her was almost unrecognizable. Akshii remembered the countless times when Mahi had given her the courage to achieve unattainble goals in impossible situations—for her the glass was never half empty.

She inched towards Mahi, trying to hug her, but as she did so, Mahi shrugged away and glared at her. She spoke through clenched teeth, 'I don't need your pity, Akshii. I can take care of myself. I made this bed and I sure can lie in it.'

'Hey, hey, hey! Nobody believes otherwise, Mahi. We just want to help. After all, that's what friends are for. Why haven't you said anything to us before, all you had to do was to pick up the phone and give us a ring,' Samrat said, wiping the tears from her face.

'How could I? I didn't want you guys to judge me. I chose him, how could I explain that to everyone? Besides, that was my whole identity—everybody has an identity in this world—I don't have anything to show for myself other than that. This was the only thing that I wanted, the only thing I was good at, and now I am failing at that too, Samrat, look at Akshii—mother of two, successful at her job, devoted wife—she has everything and does everything. I, on the other hand, have nothing apart from my title... I am Mahi Shah,' Mahi said pointing towards Akshii, who gazed at her with a sad look.

'I have nothing left in my life. I gave this relationship everything I had, even my self-respect,' Mahi said dejectedly. 'I don't know how I got here. Every morning I get up and I just want to kill myself. I have made myself invisible for so long that now even I can't see myself.'

'Mahi, please don't say that. You have been one of the fiercest women I have ever met in my life and I work in a cut-throat business. You are an inspiration to me, to all of us... I mean, you just set your eyes on something or someone and then go after it no matter who or what is in way,' Samrat said.

Mahi stared at him, forgetting everything for a moment. Akshii gave him a look which meant that he was getting himself into bigger trouble than what they were in right now.

'What the hell are you saying, Dholki?' Akshii asked him, angry.

'What I mean is that even before you became Mahi Shah and you were just Mahi, and you had everything you wanted. How can you possibly give up on that?' Samrat said.

'As much as I hate to admit it, he is right. He is stupid, no doubt about that, but right. Even before you had the Shah title you were undefeatable. Mahi, you are the strongest person I have ever met. You can't let a man, any man, defeat you. Besides, how can you admit defeat, you haven't even begun fighting,' Akshii said, smiling at her friend.

'Oh, how sweet. My heart just melted. I mean, isn't it just so beautiful?' Dorky taunted, awakening from his little daze. For a moment, as Mahi was narrating her tale, he had felt sorry for her. He didn't want to continue this any longer. He wanted to walk away—listening to Mahi's story and the sight of Kabir lying in a pool of his own blood made him want to puke. But then, when he saw Akshii and Samrat consoling Mahi, he felt betrayed. He felt abandoned by the very same people who were so eager to help out their other friends in need. Where were they when he needed them? Why weren't they at his side? Why did they let him suffer alone? The anger in him resurfaced.

'Dorky, listen, I understand how you feel. But killing us isn't the solution to this problem,' Mahi looked at him pleadingly.

'You think you know what I've been through just because your husband cheated on you. Well, that's your own fault. You could have chosen someone who loved you, rather than someone who had money. I came to you, I asked you to be with me... I loved you so much, Mahi. I always did. But you never had the time to even look at me. You exploited me. You made me do your assignments, your projects—you made me your mule—and I did it without any complaint because I loved you,' Dorky vented.

'My life is a mess, all thanks to you. Thanks to all of you. And now you want me to move on because you had a couple of hitches in your life. I loved you, Mahi!' Dorky exclaimed heatedly.

'Dorky, what is my favourite flower?' Mahi asked calmly.

'What?' Dorky asked surprised. 'Are you making fun of me?' he yelled angrily.

'No, can you please calm down and listen for a moment,' Mahi pleaded.

'Fine, but if you are, I warn you, I will ,' Dorky lashed.

'What will you do exactly? You already have the gun... what else can you do which you are not thinking about doing right now?' Krish chuckled sadly.

'Ha! I see that you've got your voice back—now cut it out and sit down.' Dorky said, waving the gun in his face and turning back to Mahi.

'What is my favourite flower, Dorky?' asked Mahi.

'Red roses,' Dorky responded, irritated and wondering to himself why he was letting himself get led into this conversation.

'No, it's rajnigandha,' said Mahi shaking her head at him. 'See, you didn't love me. All you wanted was a pin-up doll,' Mahi said, trying to explain.

'So, now you are going to tell me how I felt. Mahi, I poured out my heart in front of you and you stomped all over it. How do you think I would have felt?' Dorky said angrily.

'I am all alone! Thanks to you, I can't ever feel anything without being gripped by the fear of being rejected. It's all your fault!' Dorky yelled and pointed the gun at her once again.

≈

18

Forever Alone

DORKY EXPECTED MAHI to shut up—after all, that is what a normal person would do if a gun was being pointed straight in their direction. But this was a different Mahi…this was a Mahi who had tried killing herself thrice in the past.

With bloodshot eyes and rage in every step, Mahi walked towards Dorky as if challenging him to pull the trigger if he had the balls.

Before Dorky could react, Krish came out of nowhere and placed himself between Mahi and Dorky's blood thirsty gun.

Mahi and Dorky gazed at Krish in disbelief as they saw tears roll down his face as he spoke, 'Alone? I don't think you even understand what being alone means, Dorky. You are so consumed by your own self-pity that you never saw or understood the pain your friends went through. I am the one who is truly alone, but I cannot blame anyone else for that. My dad is gone and even when he was there, he was more of a business mentor rather than a father. Was it fair to me that my mother was gone even before I had the chance to understand what the word "mother" means? I have never experienced that kind of love, nor do I know what it feels like to have someone else sacrifice for love.'

Krish held Mahi by her arm and yanked her with such force that Dorky took a couple of nervous steps back. He continued, 'I don't think you ever loved her. For you it was always about making a trophy girlfriend out of the most beautiful girl in college. Are you wondering how I can be so sure? Well, in case you haven't noticed, when it comes to conning girls into one-night stands, I am the expert. While I may not be able to identify true love, I can identify intentions like yours with my eyes closed.

'And maybe what I am saying today makes no sense whatsoever but if you do have to kill someone, kill me. Apart from you guys, and maybe my banker, nobody will ever miss me.'

With every passing minute, Dorky's impatience was growing. Unable to control his frustration, he snapped back, 'Wow! The sinner talks like a saint. Now I have to take lessons in morality from St. Krish the Great. Fine, if you want to be the first among equals to take the bullet, so be it.'

Seeing the intent in Dorky's eyes, Krish closed his, trying to remember the almost negligible number of people who cared for him. His tears rolled down once again, this time in a continuous stream.

Seeing the situation move at hyper-speed to a dangerous and predictable end, the others froze with a sense of unease they had never experienced before. Akshii took another shot at reasoning it out with Dorky, 'Dorky, this is not you. You are better than this. We promise, we will work things out together.'

As if speaking his last words, Krish added, 'And this my friend is my personal experience—trying to hold on to something or someone to prove a point is the grand door to loneliness. All my life I've tried so hard to be the stud who could sweep women off their feet. I wanted people to envy my lifestyle and my freedom but in the process I alienated everyone.

'Promise me Dorky that after shooting me you will think for a minute about what you did. If you feel the slightest bit of remorse, please don't kill any of your other friends who have cared for you more than you know,' Krish continued.

These words from Krish were unsettling and Dorky felt like throwing up. He suddenly was at a loss for words and did not know how to respond to what he had just heard.

Suddenly, he remembered that Krish had always been a showman and for all he knew this was another one of Krish's masterpieces. This thought rekindled the hatred in Dorky and he shouted, 'Enough! I am on to your game, Krish! Did you think that I would be so stupid that I would forget that you are a genius at this game? Your plan of unsettling me is not going to work today. I am not the same Dorky I used to be ten years back. I can see through your plan, even if your friends don't. The second I decide to pull this trigger, you will be the first one running in the opposite direction.

'And just for the record, I know exactly what loneliness is. I have experienced it for ten long years, and unlike you, I did not have the money to buy friendship or loyalty. I may have fallen for this soppy crap once, but I am not dumb enough to fall for it again,' he said.

Krish looked at his friend completely flabbergasted—Dorky's reaction totally pissed him off. For the first time that evening, he didn't care that Dorky a gun in his hand, all he wanted to do was to shake him bad—shake him and make him realize that he cared about him, all of them did.

But before he could do that, a voice spoke from behind, 'Well, even if you choose not to believe him, you are still dumb. You want to shoot the only roomful of people who care about you at all. Now that's something only an acutely dumb person would do.'

'Oho, Mr Lawyer is up and chirpy!' Dorky said, his gaze shifting toward a now-conscious Kabir, forgetting all about the conversation with Krish.

Everyone sighed with relief as they saw Kabir trying to get back to his feet. Akshii ran towards him and hugged him tightly.

'You need to see a doctor,' spoke Akshii with a sense of urgency as she stopped him from getting back up on his feet.

'Dorky, just let Kabir go. We are here with you,' Dholki made a desperate attempt.

Before Dholki could speak any further, Kabir put up a hand to silence him. 'If it's about Mahi and unending love for her, how can I be left out of this story, mate?' said Kabir, finally standing up and taking two stumbling steps forward, his gaze fixed lovingly on Mahi.

≈

19

Eternally Yours

'YOU THINK YOU are the only one who loves Mahi?' Kabir spoke after an eternal silence.

'Kabir, I think you need to sit down. You are still weak and I don't think you have the strength for this,' Akshii implored as he swayed and stumbled on his feet.

'No, Akshii, not today. I finally have the strength to own up to my feelings. If I don't do it today, I will keep cursing myself for the rest of my life,' he looked at her with resolve in his eyes.

'What is he talking about?' Dorky asked intrigued.

Kabir turned towards Mahi and said, 'I too have loved Mahi from the minute I saw her on the first day of college. Since then, I have tried to gather the courage to walk up to her and tell her, but it never happened. Once I realized how happily married she was, I soothed myself by thinking that this was the happiness she deserved. I knew that marrying Sidharth was a bad decision. I knew that sooner or later Mahi's heart would be broken by his hands. But deciding that this was what she had chosen I stayed away.' Kabir hesitated, looked at Mahi's amazed expression and continued, 'Mahi, I guess this is a bit late and I don't know if it's worth anything now, but I love you. I have loved you since the moment I laid my eyes on you on the very first day of college.'

Mahi looked at him with her mouth open, totally baffled. Kabir gave her a smile and said, 'This expression, this wide-eyed innocence, is what made me fall in love with you. Maybe to everyone else you were a diva, but to me, you were someone who could never think badly about anyone.

'What a contrast Dorky. I couldn't gather up the courage to express my feelings, and here you are, all set to kill the person you claim to love so much? If you love someone you don't kill them, you save them from all pain,' said Kabir turning towards Dorky.

'Oh my god! Another sulking baby!' Dorky yelled. 'You think you and I are the same, huh, hotshot lawyer? Let's revisit this, shall we? You have always been beside Mahi like her knight in shining armour. You were the star while I was treated as the black mark that tagged along with the otherwise shining Fiasco Five. You've already had your chance.'

'But I have always cherished both your friendships equally,' chipped in Mahi, feeling a little embarrassed and enraged at the same time. Before Mahi could say another word, Dorky put a finger on his lips signalling Mahi to keep quiet.

Dorky tried the same gesture with Kabir, but Kabir was in no mood to let go, 'My life hasn't been a bed of roses either. I agree I got what I dreamt of in college—how did you put it—a hotshot legal practice, but I worked my ass off for that. Or did you think that a legal degree after college and an established practice were thrown into my lap?

'But now I realize that I was running after the wrong dream. I tried to assuage my ego by creating newer and harsher rules for my juniors, and soon I too was like a robot programmed with my own rules,' Kabir said swaying dangerously, which made Mahi run up and hold him.

He looked at her angelic face which was covered with lines of worry and concern and wondered how he could have ever given up on her. He brushed a lock of hair away from her face and said, 'I was running around focusing on the wrong things, when I should have just focused on her. All through my college years, I kept looking for the perfect moment to muster my courage and tell her my feelings, but I failed to recognize that every moment with her was the perfect one. So, here goes— Mahi, you are the love of my life. I have loved you since the very first moment I laid eyes on you and will always love you till my very last breath, which of course, if Dorky has his way, won't be very long from now.'

Despite the tension in the air, all of them chuckled and shook their heads in disbelief that even in a situation like this he was cracking jokes. He smiled as he stood hugging Mahi, until Mahi spoke with a guilty look on her face, 'Kabir, I need to say something.'

'No, no. Don't say anything, Mahi. I know it's too late now. You are happily married. Look, I didn't tell you about my feelings because I expected nothing back from you. I shouldn't have brought it up,' Kabir spoke before Mahi could utter another word while Dorky raised his eyebrows in disbelief.

'Kabir, will you let me speak please? Trust me, you would want to hear me out,' Mahi said as Kabir started to object again. He looked at her quizzically while Mahi beamed at him and said, 'Kabir, I love you, too. In fact, I have loved you since college but I just figured that if you had felt the same way you would have said something or even hinted at it.'

'What?' spoke all of them in unison.

'You loved me?' Kabir asked surprised, 'But...but then why didn't you say something?'

'Did you know about this?' Krish leaned in and whispered to Akshii, who looked as stunned as the others, if possible, more so.

'No, not in the least, or else I would've done something about it. I just knew that he liked her, that's all. I kept asking him to say something to her,' Akshii whispered back.

Both Krish and Samrat spun around and asked loudly, 'You knew?'

'What?' asked Mahi, as she and Kabir broke from their trance and looked at them.

'She knew?' asked Krish in an accusatory voice while Samrat looked viciously at Kabir.

'What are you guys talking about?' Mahi asked, giving all three of them a confused look.

'Akshii knew about Kabir's feelings,' Krish sounded like a little boy who was complaining about his older sibling to his mom.

'What? You knew? Why didn't you say anything?' Mahi asked amused.

Akshii looked at Krish with murder in her eyes, 'Thanks, Krish.' And then she added defensively, looking at Mahi, 'Well, you never gave me any hint that you liked him. How in the world was I supposed to know about it?'

Mahi piped down and asked, 'Since when have you known?'

'Since the start of our second year, when he got you that

ridiculously expensive birthday cake which was shaped like that teddy bear of yours,' Akshii answered.

'She knew even before we knew? You didn't tell us till the end of our third year!'

Kabir shifted uncomfortably under their gazes and said defensively, 'Hey, I didn't tell her anything. She guessed it herself—and FYI—I still have no idea how she did it. She came to me and asked me point blank; what was I supposed to do?'

'Oh please! You roamed around the whole city trying to find her a teddy bear which looked like the one she had as a child. When you couldn't, you went to a five-star hotel's patisserie and got a 3-kg double chocolate cake with white chocolate icing made. And that too, for a party of six people, Kabir,' Akshii retorted with a snort as if it was the most obvious thing in the world.

'Hang on a minute. So let me get this straight. Everyone knew that Kabir liked me, apart from me. I can't believe this,' Mahi said in disbelief.

'I should've listened to you all those years ago. It would have saved me years of heartbreak,' Kabir said hugging Akshii.

Akshii looked at Mahi excitedly and said, 'Mahi, now you know. I can't believe this! My two best friends are getting together!'

'No, we are not,' Mahi said in a quiet voice. The smiles vanished from everyone's faces except from Kabir's.

Akshii asked agitatedly, 'What? Why, Mahi? You know that your husband is a cheating bastard who doesn't deserve you. And Kabir... Mahi, he loves you so much and you love him too. So, why not? And you, Kabir, why aren't you saying anything? Guys do something, say something.'

Before any of them could intervene, Kabir raised a hand indicating that they should stay quiet. He stood beside Mahi and said, 'Akshii, I didn't say anything expecting Mahi to be with me. Whether she wants to be with me or not, can only be her prerogative.'

'Actually, whether she is going to be with you or not is my prerogative,' Dorky yelled suddenly and everyone flinched remembering the situation they were in.

He smiled crazily and said, 'Remember me—the guy with the gun?' and waved it in the air.

Already agitated, Akshii broke away from everyone and said, 'Dorky, c'mon, don't you feel for your friends at all? You are not a monster.'

'It's easy for you to say this. He gets the girl, you have a family, Samrat has his success and well, Krish just has everything. But what about me? I am all alone and all I want is to get away from this emptiness which has engulfed my life,' Dorky exploded.

20

Best Mom Syndrome

'YOU THINK BEING with someone makes you complete—I have news for you—sometimes being alone is the best thing in the world. You think my life is perfect with a beautiful family and a nice job, I mean what else could I ever want from life? You want to know what I want—me! You have no idea what it takes to manage a job and a child and a husband all at the same time,' Akshii said, tired.

'Don't look at me like that. It's exhausting being there for everyone. My kid, my job, my husband, all of them expect something out of me and you know what happens when I am not able to fulfil those expectations? I blame myself. All my life I worked hard so that my kid won't resent me as I resented my parents. But no matter what I do I just can't get it right. I resented my parents for taking decisions for me, for thinking what would be best for me and in the process forgetting to ask me what I wanted. I promised to myself then that I would lead my life the way I wanted and not by the norms set by anyone only to realize that I am stuck in the same circle again,' Akshii rambled, looking at her friends.

'Nobody cares about what I want. Hell, even I don't care any more about what I want. A while back I thought that my husband was cheating on me and do you know what I felt? Relieved! I was relieved that he wouldn't expect anything out of me for some time. But even that was all in my head,' Akshii said shaking her head painfully.

'The truth is, Dorky, we have no idea what we want. All of us are running in circles trying to catch those little pieces that we call life. People say life begins when you have someone to share it with, then they say it's when you have a child, and then they say that your child is your life. But it actually starts when you decide to let it start,' Akshii spoke with tears glistening in her eyes.

'So you mean to say that I haven't decided to start my life. Is that what are you saying? Because it's really that simple, isn't it?' asked Dorky

'What do you want from us, Dorky?' Akshii asked tired.

'What's the matter with you?' Krish asked unbelievingly. 'At first I thought you were just angry at us, but all you care about is your stupid grudge which happened like a gazillion years ago.'

'Just shut the fuck up,' Dorky yelled, trying to take control of the situation which was spiralling into chaos. This was not how he had planned it. He had planned on them cowering in fear, begging for their lives. He wanted to feel the power and control over their lives, the power and control which he never had over his own life.

'No, I have had enough of this, Dork. He is right—didn't you hear us or are you so mesmerised by your own pain that you are unable to see that each one of us has had to deal with our fair share of it as well? That's what it's all about—who said that life's gonna be easy? No, seriously, just point me towards that sick bastard and I will shoot him for you,' Akshii yelled. 'You know, before I came here, I was so happy for tonight. This was the first time in years when I was doing something for myself. Just me—no husband, no child—but you screwed it up!'

'I ruined your night? Are you kidding me? You're actually blaming me for one night, when you guys have royally screwed up my life? It stings doesn't it, when you imagine something in a certain way but it turns out to be the complete opposite? It infuriates you to think that someone you counted as a friend and wanted support from, just abandoned you. Now imagine my life, a constant source of disappointment...all my life I worked harder than all of you. My scholarship was stolen away from me, the girl that I loved insanely kept toying with my emotions, my own friends decided, I wasn't even worth it,' Dorky yelled.

'Disappointment? Really, Dorky? Don't talk to me about disappointment until you have looked into the eyes of your four-year-old kid who is hugging you and asking you to stay with him while you are walking out of your home every morning. Disappointment is when no matter how hard you try, you can never be there for your child's first stage performance or even to tuck him into bed every night. Disappointment is when your child runs into the arms of his nanny when he is hurt, while you are standing right beside him. Disappointment is when your husband looks at you and you know that all he is thinking about is when you will be back today,' Akshii said with feelings pouring out of her.

'And you think we abandoned you? We went insane trying to get you to talk to us, but you were so angry, you wanted us to leave you. Isn't it? Remember the last conversation we had in college? You asked me whether I ever thought of you as a friend and whether I could understand what you must be going through then I should let you go through it alone.' Akshii said with such convivtion that her whole body trembled.

Dorky looked at her at a loss for words, and for the first time since he had entered the classroom, doubted himself and his actions.

'Do you know what the biggest disappointment in life is? When no matter what you do or don't do, you can't find yourself. This evening wasn't important because I was without my husband or child, but it was important because I thought that if there was anyone in the whole world who could help me find myself, it would be the people in this room—my friends.'

Akshii walked to him, put one hand on his shoulder and said, 'Dorky, life is full of difficult decisions, but it takes shape by what you decide and what choices you make. Mine went wrong when I decided to take up everything and became worse when I gave my job and my family equal importance and yours....'

'And mine went wrong when I blamed you guys, isn't that what you were going to say?' Dorky asked, slapping her hand away angrily.

'No, not at all. I was going to say that yours went wrong when you let that one day get the best of you,' Akshii said in disbelief. She looked at her friend, who no matter what she said, wasn't willing to believe her. She leaned forward and said pleadingly, 'Dorky, all I'm trying to say is that just like me you have lost yourself too. This is not my friend, the guy I knew was the sweetest person who cared about everything and everyone, and never even thought about harming a fly. This is not you.

And we can help you, just give us another chance.'

'Another chance? What good would it do? You are right Akshii, this is not me. This is what your choices have made me,' Dorky said pointing towards the gun in his hand. 'I changed the day I was willing to pull the trigger on myself. What good did being sweet do for me? Everyone stepped on me and moved on with their lives, but I was left right where I was ten years ago, with a broken heart and a broken spirit.' He sighed, raised the gun once more, and said, 'So here I am.'

Akshii looked into his eyes, searching, and then with deep resolve stood right in front of the gun. 'Fine, Dorky. If killing us will give you the strength to move on, or even let you die peacefully, then start with me because I can't stand seeing my friends lost forever.'

Dorky looked at Akshii who didn't budge, though the others shouted around them and Kabir struggled with Krish and Samrat who were trying to hold him back. Dorky looked at his own hand which was shaking tremendously. After what seemed like eternity in which he willed himself to pull the trigger, he yelled incoherently 'ARRRRRGHHHHHHHHHH' and put his hand down saying, 'I can't do this, just get out of here, all of you. Go away. Just leave me alone!'

Akshii immediately hugged him, 'Dorky, it's okay. Calm down.'

Dorky struggled to break loose of Akshii's embrace and said, 'Just go away before I change my mind. I don't want to see any of you ever again.'

Samrat approached him saying, 'We did that once and look where it got us. We are to blame for that—we gave up on you when we should have fought harder to be with you. I'm never giving up on you again and I'm afraid that means that we're not leaving unless you come with us. I am so sorry that you had to go through everything alone. But I am not going through my life feeing sorry to have left you alone now'

Dorky said, '*Now* you are sorry, when we have reached this point. Were you sorry when you stole my scholarship? Were you sorry when you were busy living my life...? Did you remember even once that you had stepped on your friend to get where you are? You got all you ever wanted.'

Kabir came thundering forward and pushed Dorky away, saying, 'There is no point explaining anything to you. That's your problem, once you make up your mind about something, you never listen to anything. The college gave him the scholarship; why and how was it his fault? He should have rejected the scholarship saying, "Oh no, I don't want this scholarship even though I know I will not be able to afford further education without it. But who cares about my future, I have a friend who wanted this, and although he might never get it, I can't accept it."'

Samrat caught Kabir's arm yelling, 'What the hell, Kabir? Will you please be quiet for some time, I am trying to talk to him and I don't need you to further complicate things. So for now, will you please go back and be quiet?'

As Kabir turned and walked away angrily, he look at Dorky one last time, who looked shaken himself.

≈

21

Fallen Prince

SAMRAT WINCED AND looked at Dorky. With his heart in his mouth, he took a deep breath and said, 'Everything I did, I did for my family. Dorky, my whole life I just saw need, poverty and no means to fulfil them. But today, the people for whom I had done it are not with me. My wife resents me and my kid doesn't even know how to talk to me.

'At least you can blame your husband, Mahi, and Dorky, you might blame me. But let me tell you that whatever blame you might put on me is nothing compared to the blame I put on myself. You say I have ruined your life, but how could I? I was too busy screwing up my own,' Samrat said chuckling painfully.

'Just like you, I thought money would solve all my problems. That was the one thing I had never had, and I foolishly thought that it could buy satisfaction, but no, all it bought was discontent. The more I earned the more I ran after it, until I was obsessed with it. The sad part is, before we stepped into this classroom, I still believed that it was Karuna's fault,' he continued, wincing with every word.

'Can you believe it? Even now, all I wanted to do was to prove that she was wrong and I was right. Maybe I didn't cheat on her, but what difference does it make, when I single-handedly screwed it all up. Am I to blame any less than Mahi's husband? Didn't I hurt my wife in the same way? I came here tonight because I thought that if I rescheduled my work for my friends and somehow came here it would prove once and for all that what I was doing wasn't selfish. That when I need to be there and when important events in my life happened I was there. I don't give preference to work over my life. I wanted to believe so desperately that she was the one who was being unreasonable, and for what? For wanting me to give some time to her, be a part of my kid's life, and god forbid, myself and my hobbies,' he said unbelievingly.

'Samrat, please stop badgering yourself. You are doing the best you can. All you wanted was to control your life,' Krish said, wondering what else to say to him.

Samrat looked at him and continued, 'Control what, Krish? Let me speak, because then at least everything will be out in the open. How am I different from your father? All your life you have resented him for the very same reason—he was never there— just like I have never been there for my kid. You know people say that when they hold their kids for the first time, everything changes and they completely shuffle their lives around them. But what did I do? Nothing... I didn't even see my kid for the first five days.'

'Don't say that, Samrat. You are different! I know that when you get out of this room you will put everything back in its right place,' Krish said vehemently.

'How can you say that with such conviction, Krish?' Samrat

said. 'What if I can never do that? What if I can never glue my family back? What if…?'

'Hey, hey! Stop! Samrat, I know it because I know you. Look at you. I know that you will not be able to breathe normally until you make everything right. Even if you don't admit it, your family is the most important thing in your life. Also, if you don't, I will personally kick your ass. Heck, all of us will do that. That is, if we ever make out of here alive,' Krish said, making a weak joke.

Dorky looked at Dholki and saw his own pain reflected in his face. He did not know anymore what he felt. All he knew was that the pain that all of them were going through was no less than his own.

He looked at all their faces and the gravity of the situation—the gravity of his decision and his actions—dawned on him. He stumbled backwards in horror.

'Dorky!' yelled all of them, concerned.

'Please, just leave me alone,' Dorky said, trying to create some space between them. He could not stand the concern in their eyes—he could have understood their anger, even their silence, but the concern in their eyes was unbearable.

He winced at the thought of what could have happened, and guilt rose up in him. He backed away to the corner of the room trying to vanish from their collective gaze. Krish walked towards him cautiously, as if he was approaching a skittish animal, and said, 'Dorky, will you please talk to us. I can see you tormenting yourself… Will you please let us help you?'

'He is right, Damodar. All of us know now that we need each other to survive. And if you shut us out once again, it will just be wrong… C'mon, if this night has taught us anything, it's that we all need each other,' Samrat pleaded.

Akshii nudged Kabir to say something, but he shrugged indicating that he didn't have anything to say. Akshii rolled her eyes knowing that it would take some time for Kabir to see Dorky as his friend again. She knew that as much as he would give up his life for his friends, once his trust was shattered it would take a long time to build it back. Ironically, Akshii didn't think he was angry because Dorky shot him, it was probably because of the danger that Dorky had put all of them in.

Pushing all that away, she knew that right now she needed to convince Dorky to let them be a part of his life; she could already see him disintegrating in front of her eyes. If Dorky left now, he would continue to suffer in silence somewhere, and that would break her heart. She forced that image out of her mind and decided that she would not let that happen to him.

'Dorky, that's enough. We're getting out of this stupid room. Come on,' Mahi said, dragging him by his hand. 'Move guys, I've had enough,' she said as she dragged him towards the door, but Dorky dug in his heels and pulled his hand away with a jerk.

Mahi turned around with anger in her eyes and started to say, 'Dorky, look I've had enough, either you come with me or…,' but stopped, with a gasp, as she saw him standing in the middle of the room pointing the gun.

Everyone's heart skipped a beat as they saw Dorky pull the gun up once again, but this time he pointed it at his temple. He gave all of them a tearful look and said guiltily, 'I am not going anywhere, I made that decision the moment I pulled this gun on you guys.'

'Dorky, are you mad? Put the gun down. You still have so much to look forward to. Besides, none of us think this is entirely your fault,' Akshii said with a tremble in her voice.

'No, even if you guys don't blame me, I will never be able to live with the guilt. What the hell was I thinking? You and Samrat have kids, I didn't even think about them,' Dorky said with resolve in his voice.

'Well, you weren't thinking... That's exactly what we are saying, Dorky. But think now, please, and drop that gun. Let's get out of this room. I've had quite enough learning for one night. I get that you're feeling guilty, but the fact is that all of us had some part to play in today's mishap. Just give it a thought and stop feeling guilty. We do not blame you for anything. Trust me. Trust us,' Samrat implored.

'Yes, for once I think I am thinking clearly,' Dorky said silently as he closed his eyes, brought the gun to his temple and pulled the trigger.

≈

22

That's How the Cookie Crumbles

AKSHII OPENED HER eyes, and realized that she was holding her breath. She saw Kabir grasping Dorky's arm, holding it as though he had just knocked it upwards. Dorky slid down onto his knees and broke into sobs. Kabir spoke with a weak voice, 'Damodar, stop it. Please.'

'Why in the world did you stop me? I am worthless. I blamed you for my failures. I can't believe what I wanted to do. How could I?' Dorky wailed.

'But nobody got hurt, Dorky. We are all fine,' Mahi said, trying to calm him down. Dorky looked up at her with guilt-ridden eyes and broke down again.

Akshii, who could have handled the screaming and anger of her friend, did not have any clue how to respond to his grief. She knelt down beside him, held his hand and said, 'You don't want to do this. C'mon, this isn't you. We don't care what happened between all of us tonight, do we guys?'

'No.' 'Not at all,' they spoke in unison.

'How can you guys not care that I tried to kill you? I could have injured Kabir...,' Dorky said tragically. 'Guys please don't be so nice to me. I do not deserve this. I deserve to go to hell, I deserve to go to jail.'

'We are not doing it for you, we are doing it for us, Dorky. We already let ten years pass without you in our lives and we aren't going to let it happen again,' Krish thumped his back and hugged him.

'Besides, jail is going to be easy. If you want punishment, then you need to promise us that you will not shut us out ever again no matter what the problem. In fact, I want that promise from all of you. I don't want any one of us to pull a Dorky ever again,' Akshii said grinning.

'Pull a what?' Samrat asked confused.

'You know, if "I am going down I will take everybody down."' Akshii said matter-of-factly making air quotes.

Dorky looked up and grimaced.

'Oh, c'mon! You know we are going to make jokes about this for the remainder of your life, don't you?' Akshii said with an evil grin, and all of them laughed looking at Dorky's expression.

'Guys... I am...,' Dorky tried to speak but was quickly silenced by everyone's groans.

Kabir said, 'Dorky, we get it. You were angry, you wanted to kill us, you tried, you felt what you were doing was wrong, you said you were sorry, we forgave you. Will you please get over it? Now can we all go before I actually have to kick your ass? We might be just in time for the goodbyes... I can't believe so much time has passed.'

'Well, when you are facing your inner chaos, time kind of takes a backseat. Besides, we can't go back there looking like this, especially you, Kabir. And not to mention, Dorky looks like he is going to burst out a river,' Akshii pointed out.

'You know what, I have had enough of this reunion. What do you guys say to going back to my hotel? I have a suite booked and I am sure they can put up a couple of extra beds. We can all sit back, freshen up and order some room service,' Krish asked tiredly.

'Oh yeah, that sounds like a great idea. I could do with a couple of plates of french fries and a fluffy bathrobe,' Mahi said hugging Kabir.

'Wow, things are pretty serious. Mahi just said she's gonna eat carbs,' Akshii said pinching her arm.

'Won't it be rude? I mean, can we leave without even saying goodbye?' Samrat said, confused.

'Who cares, they already think we are world-class jerks. I don't think I have it in me to go and be stared at anymore. And my gown is all torn up. I can't go back in looking all dishevelled,' Mahi exclaimed.

'For once I am with Mahi, I really can't put up a face. We aren't going to meet them for another ten years—Samrat, you can apologise to them then,' Akshii said, grabbing his hand and tugging on it.

'Fine, let's go,' Samrat said, resigning.

'Great, I will ask my chauffeur to bring the car out,' Mahi chirped.

Krish, meanwhile, unlatched the door and finally opened it. He took a deep breath as the fresh chilly air swept into the room. As he stepped out, he could not help but realize that a second life had begun for all of them. He realized how life itself had given them all a new beginning—it was up to them to carve it into what they wanted it to be.

As they walked towards the car, Akshii brooded about what to do next. Once they reached it, she called out from behind, 'Why don't the guys take Krish's car, it will give you some time to bitch and talk about all the women you saw today. We will have some time for some girl talk as well.'

'What kind of girl talk?' Kabir asked, sleazily gesturing with his eyebrows.

Akshii gave him a honey-dipped smile and said, 'It's NTBT.' Both of them laughed as the guys rolled their eyes, groaning. Mahi winked at them playfully as both of them climbed into her car.

Once inside, Akshii picked up a cute and cuddly cushion lying on the car seat and started hitting Mahi until she yelled, 'Akshii! What the hell? Ouch, stop! You are hurting me and destroying what's left of my hair.'

'Hurting you? Really? What the hell, Mahi? You know, I could just kill you, and trust me, if you had hurt yourself, I would definitely have killed you,' Akshii retorted.

Mahi smiled weakly and sighed looking at her friend, 'I know. And before you say it, I know that if I had called, you would have left everything to be at my side in a heartbeat.'

'Then why didn't you?' Akshii asked, suddenly changing her stance as she saw tears glistening in her friend's eyes and softly stroked her hand.

'I guess I was scared that if I said it out loud—even to you—it would make it all real. I just wouldn't be able to ignore it or run away from it. Quitting just seemed so much easier,' she spoke with a pained look on her face.

'Oh, sweetheart! You know I would never have forgiven myself if anything had happened to you. Every time I needed something you were always there. Whenever I had to make a difficult decision in my life I would always ask myself, "What would Mahi do?" And to find out that you were thinking about quitting—Mahi that's not you. I mean, the Mahi I knew is worth hundreds of Sidharths. You are a rockstar, Mahi, and if you don't believe me, ask my son who drew your stick figure as one, courtesy your leather pants-era pictures,' Akshii smiled mischievously.

Both of them laughed, tearfully, till they were breathless. Once they stopped, Mahi gazed out the window and took a deep breath. After a very long time, she was able to breathe freely. Finally tearing her gaze away from the beautiful moon, she turned to tell her friend that no matter the heartache tonight had brought, she was really grateful that it had happened. She stopped before the words could reach her lips, as she saw that her friend was fast asleep with the most peaceful look on her face.

≈

23

The Silver Lining

'OH MY GOD, these are amazing! I can't believe that I've not eaten one of these for the last six years! I could just kick myself, and trust me, I do power yoga every day; if I tried I could literally kick myself,' Mahi sputtered as she relished her second plate of french fries. 'Oh my god, Akshii, you have got to try these! They are A-M-A-Z-I-N-G! I can eat like a million of these!'

'Yeah, looks like you are definitely going to eat a million of them. Weren't there, like, four plates for the six of us?' Akshii spoke drying her hair with a towel. She joined her friends, who like her had freshened up and were now either sitting or lying down on the mattresses on the floor.

'Can we order some more?' Mahi spoke through a stuffed mouth.

'No!' Akshii and Kabir spoke together. Akshii looked at Kabir and smiled at him. He was wearing a bathrobe. His wound had just been cleaned and stitched up by the hotel doctor who promised not to say anything courtesy the huge 'tip' Krish had handed him.

Mahi made a face and returned to her plate, which made all of them laugh. Samrat turned to Dorky, who was looking at them with an unbelieving look on his face, and said hesitatingly, 'Damodar, listen, why don't you join my company? Before you say anything, just hear me out. There's a position open and we were actually looking for someone just like you, so why not you?'

'What? No, no. Damodar just say no, you will die of boredom in his company, and I don't mean the place where he works,' Krish teased. 'Besides, you are going to join me in my business. God knows it needs someone with brains. It's a surprise it hasn't collapsed already. So, what do you say?'

Dorky smiled and shook his head. He tried to speak, but was too overwhelmed to say anything. He took a couple of deep breaths, but when he spoke, his voice quivered with emotion, 'Guys, all my life I have been blaming others, especially you guys, my own friends, for everything that went wrong. I refused to take any blame myself, because blaming you was so much simpler. After eons I have finally come back to my senses. Trust me when I say this, I have absolutely no idea how to get my life back in shape, but I know that I need to pick up all the pieces myself and fix it. So, I am sorry, but I will have to decline both of your offers. Don't get me wrong, it's not that I don't need you guys because I absolutely do, but not to clean up my mess. I need you to be there as my friends, as my cheerleaders when I fall, to give me that pep talk when I lose my energy, to make me get up and fight when I say I have had enough. I need you guys for all of this, but this, this I need to do myself.' He looked at the awestruck faces of his friends and his smile broadened.

'Dorky, you are gonna make us all cry,' Mahi spoke with tears glistening in her eyes.

'Speak for yourself, we are men, we are not emotional nincompoops like girls,' Krish spoke, thumping his chest like a chimp in vain attempt to hide the moisture in his eyes.

Samrat and Kabir thumped Dorky's back while Akshii leaned in to plant a kiss on his forehead. 'Dorky, I am super proud of you. But always remember, we are here for you. Anytime you need.'

'Enough about me! Please stop. What are you going to do, Akshii?' Dorky exclaimed, trying to change the topic.

'Well, I don't know—but one thing I do know is that if I become a stay-at-home mom, my kid is pretty soon going to kill me,' Akshii said, chuckling. 'Actually, there was an offer sometime back. It's a little less money but the working hours are flexible and it also involves lesser hours of travelling. I rejected it before, but I am sure I can approach them to initiate the offer once again.'

'Why did you reject it before? Was the job not satisfying enough?' Kabir asked.

'No, it's not that. It's just that I invested so much of myself in this job, it just felt like a part of me. But each time I see disappointment in my child's eyes, it chips away a part of my heart and soul. Instead of beating myself up every time, I think it would be better to give a higher priority to my family right now. Before tonight, I was very conflicted about this decision. I thought that this job was my complete identity, and if I gave it up I would lose myself. But I realized today that the most important thing in my life is my family and I can do anything for them. Comparing them to a job is just petty,' Akshii said, pouring out her mind. Mahi gave her a huge hug while the others smiled.

'Okay guys, it's gotten a little too soppy in here. Before we all start bawling like little girls, can we sleep, please? I don't know about you guys, but I am unable to keep my eyes open,' Krish mumbled, rubbing his eyes with the back of his hand. 'Akshii, you and Mahi can take the room, and all of us guys can camp out here. What say?' Krish spoke yawning, and everybody nodded along.

As they all got up to take their respective places, Kabir spoke suddenly, 'Actually Mahi, can we talk?' which was followed by a series of ooh's by the others, and Krish singing, 'Kabir and Mahi sitting in a tree, K-I-S-S-I-N-G!'

Kabir narrowed his eyes which made everybody suddenly remember they had something to do. But as soon as they turned around to walk to the balcony, they heard giggling and shushing from behind.

Once outside, Kabir gulped and looked at Mahi, who was gazing at the twinkling lights of the city. 'Wow, the way my heart is thumping right now, it feels as if I am having a heart attack. Argh, I am thirty-three years old, and I have a law firm for crying out loud; this should be easy. Instead, I feel like a stupid teenager.'

Mahi smiled, blushing, and looked deep into his eyes. 'Kabir, before you say anything, I just want to tell you that no matter what my husband has done, I can't cheat on him. Don't get me wrong, I'm not going to stay with him. In fact, I am going to file for divorce first thing when I reach home. But you should know, until that happens, I can't be with you.'

Kabir laughed, 'Hey, hey, hey, I know. Even if you hadn't said this, I knew you wouldn't have done anything. And even if you would have, I wouldn't have let you. I love you, Mahi.

Always have, always will. But I don't want you to be divided. I have waited this long, I can wait for you a little more... How about my whole life?'

'But it's a long time, Kabir. A lot of things change—I don't want you to resent me or wake up one day and regret your decision. Besides, it's not that simple. I still need to figure out my life. I don't want you to feel that you're Plan B. I want to be with you because it's going to make me happy, not because I just need someone to help me clean up my life,' Mahi spoke, emotions pouring into every syllable.

'Shhh...Mahi. Relax. Just breathe for a minute,' Kabir spoke, taking her into his arms. 'Mahi, I don't care how long I need to wait. I don't care how much time you need, heck, I don't even care if you decide not to be with me. Don't you get it— all I want is to be a part of your life, no matter how small. If you are happy, that's all I care about. I walked away from your life because I couldn't stand seeing you hurt yourself, which I knew would happen if you chose Sidharth. That was my fault, I should have fought for you, but instead, I just gave up. If something had happened to you, I don't know what I would have done. But one thing I do know, I would not have been able to smile ever again.'

'Kabir, I...,' Mahi looked into his eyes as she tried to speak, but was shushed when Kabir embraced her tighter.

She looked at his beautiful face smiling down at her and cursed herself for being so dumb— she had lost precious time with the one person she was probably destined to be with, all because of her superficial dreams. She knew that the path she had chosen now would not be easy, but she would conquer it. She would figure out her life and then she would come back to this very place because she knew now that this was her destiny. Mahi closed her eyes and nuzzled up against him; for a moment she forgot about everything and all her worries washed away. Somehow, this felt right, it felt safe. Steeling herself, she broke away from his embrace because if she didn't, she knew she would just melt.

'Okay guys, can we come out there, our ears hurt, and we really, really want to,' Krish spoke peering through the place where they were all hidden.

Kabir groaned and rolled his eyes while Mahi shook her head in incredulity. 'Yeah, sure. Although if you don't wake up tomorrow morning, don't blame me,' Kabir said.

They came out with wine in their hands, giggling and teasing, while Kabir and Mahi blushed uncontrollably. Akshii rushed to Mahi's side and hugged her, giving her a glass. As all of them took turns to congratulate them, Akshii whispered something in Mahi's ears which made both of them laugh hysterically.

Everyone else's ears perked up, and they looked at them with suspicion. 'What...what happened? What did you say? Why are you guys laughing? Is it something we said?'

Both the girls laughed out once again, enjoying their misery all the more. Rubbing salt on the wound, Akshii spoke with her most evil grin, 'It's NTBT!'

The guys groaned. 'Not that stupid crap again. For god's sake, it's been ten long years, will you please tell us what that means? We have tried every permutation and combination, but we don't get it.'

Mahi grinned and said, 'We will, if you accept that girls are better than boys... You don't even have to say it, just give a nod.' Akshii laughed at the expressions on their faces as they wondered whether to accept defeat or give in to their curiosity.

Giving up, Krish, representing the guys, said, 'Girls are so much better than boys. Your gender is more intelligent, beautiful and sensitive than ours. So, if our ladyships would be kind enough to enlighten us with their secret, we would be indebted to you forever.'

Both of them chuckled together and said, 'NTBT means Not To Be Told.' They laughed loudly as the guys smacked their heads.

As they laughed and teased each other, Krish looked around at the faces of his friends. He was sure of one thing—the chaos within them was finally put to rest.

Acknowledgements

Thanks to everyone who has put up with me and made me my whacky, quirky self. You all know who you are. Stay crazy.

Hats off to my parents—you have put up with my craziness for the longest, but before you feel too exhilarated just remember I get it from both of you, so thanks for that. And an even bigger hats off to my in-laws who have welcomed all my craziness in their lives with utmost love.

Thanks to my not-so-little brother, who inspired me to start reading books by breaking all my toys, and who, at the tender age of two, had such big plans for me.

A big thanks to Rupa Publications and its awesome team for showing immense faith in me.

P.S.: If after reading the novel you find a character too similar to yourself, it probably is. So thanks for that.